MW00815007

A Life, APart

Cynthia Strauff

Copyright 2020 by Cynthia Strauff

A Life, APart is a work of fiction set in an historical context. Any resemblance to persons living or dead is entirely coincidental.

ISBN: 978-1-71662-956-3

ISBN: (e) 978-1-71661-297-8

Library of Congress Control Number: 2020917116

The First Chapter

It was in her mind before she woke, always there, just under the surface. Viktor had wanted to stay, but she wanted this last night to herself. "We've spent enough nights together," she told him. "Let's remember those. This, well, this would only make the memory, the last memory, sad. And we've had enough of that for this life, don't you think?

He had taken her hand and kissed it, then left without saying another word.

He would arrive, earlier, she knew, than they had agreed upon. She was grateful for that. She rose, splashed cold water on her face, then looked in the mirror and laughed. She smoothed her eyebrows. Today I'm looking pretty good. It figures. She said these last two words aloud, and was glad.

She took care when she dressed, chose a favorite black cashmere sweater, although black was not the most becoming color for her these days; a pleated Stewart-tartan skirt, complete with oversized safety pin, a bit too young for her, a bit too big on her now slight frame. But it was a favorite. And black hose, black patent-leather flats, with a black grosgrain bow. Yes, this was how she wanted to look. She brushed her hair back, and with all that had befallen her, still mourned that it was no longer thick, that, if she looked, she could see her skull. What does Viktor see, she wondered, and then closed her eyes.

She wanted to be fully present this day, to experience this day, with Viktor. Books, music, they had spent many of their precious hours planning it. And ice cream, Hendler's Vanilla Bean, topped with bourbon. She had planned; all that needed to be taken care of was taken care of. No loose ends, no one to leave them to anyway, except Viktor. He would handle what needed to be handled.

He arrived, an hour earlier than they had agreed upon. He always knocked, three rapid raps, before he used the key he had possessed for years. His favorite books, favorite records already part of her, their, collection.

1

They sat through the afternoon, left the lamps unlit as the evening came, nursed their drinks, from habit. Their ritual, important on this day, to both. They read, each with their own thoughts, but close, sitting close, on the sofa. Later Claire lay, her head in Viktor's lap as he stroked her forehead. She reached for his hand and placed it on her chest.

"It's time, I think." She spoke without looking at him, and started to sit up.

He helped her as she raised her head, her shoulders, from his lap. "I need to tell you," he said, as he leaned her body against his. "I'm going with you. We'll do this together." He put his fingers to her lips. "Don't waste, don't use your energy talking about this. If you are not here, then I have no life, no life that I am interested in living. How many deaths have I escaped? This is one I don't want to. We'll go. We'll go together."

Claire shook her head. "Agata. What about Agata?" She was so tired, couldn't muster up energy to say words she knew should be said.

"Agata. Another sad soul. But she knew, from the beginning she knew. And decided on what she wanted. Another broken soul, Claire, just one more. She will be relieved, I think. This has been no life for her, not really. She has friends, people who love her. They'll make her life better." Viktor took her hand, kissed it. "She knew, Claire. She always knew."

They sat, each with only thoughts; words insufficient, or unnecessary, now. She knew, Claire thought. Yes, she knew. And Viktor, my love, will do exactly as he chooses. I was, I am his love, she thought. Yes, it is I.

They walked to the bedroom, Viktor steadying her gait. He helped her onto the bed, straightened the coverlet, fluffed the pillows behind her. She reached into the drawer of the bedside table, pulled out the containers of sleeping pills. She had been accumulating them for months. "I think ice cream now. Would you fix it?"

2

Viktor went into the kitchen, spooned two scoops into the two bowls Claire had chosen, emptied the capsules and added enough morphine to do what it was meant to do. He added a spoonful of bourbon to each, for taste, and the memory.

Returning, he handed one dish to Claire, then got into bed on his customary side. After a few bites, Claire looked over. "Make sure I get all this down." She paused. "I know this is the right thing for me, the right ending." She stared into the bowl. "And you? Are you sure?"

Viktor smiled, scraped the last of the liquid onto his spoon.

"Now don't forget to wash the bowls and put them in the dish drainer."

Viktor smiled. "Ah, yes. We will follow our plan."

"And make sure that we're sitting up. In case things get messy. I would hate that."

"No worry. No worry. My Clairedelune."

He returned from the kitchen and took her hand. Her breathing had slowed; he knew his would soon follow suit.

"But who will be the executor? Who will take care of all the details? We shouldn't leave that to Harriet. It isn't fair. I, we, haven't prepared her for this."

Viktor took her hand, leaned to kiss her forehead. "Oh, my Clairedelune. Some things you just have to leave to chance."

Claire smiled and closed her eyes, feeling her hand in his, and thought of Viktor, of Fritz, of Lily, of Sylvan Cliffs, and General.

Part One

One

Tuesday

Claire shifted from one foot to the other waiting for the fire-engine red pick-up truck. But it was the maroon Packard that made its way south on Charles Street to turn onto Mt. Vernon Place. She leaned against the cold grey stone of the Peabody Preparatory building, and frowned as the car turned the corner and made its way down the steep hill.

She tapped at the window on the driver's side. "Where's Faht? I thought he was picking me up." Her mother rolled down the window and started to speak. Claire interrupted her. "No matter," she said. "I'll drive, Mamma, let me drive. Slide over. Please, for me. Who's just had a great piano lesson?" She laughed and started to open the driver's side door.

Lily waved her hand. "No, I don't want to move; this skirt will wrinkle even more than it has. You just get in the other side."

Claire rolled her eyes. She wanted, needed, driving practice. Crossing in front of the car, she threw her satchel onto the back seat. The loosely-fastened clasp opened, and textbooks, papers, music scores spilled onto the floor and under the seat. Claire leaned over to kiss her mother.

Lily smiled. "Hello, sweetness. Faht's meeting Uncle August for an early dinner, so it's you and me."

"I like that, spending time with you. We can talk," Claire responded She shifted in her seat to face her mother. "Now, what should we talk about?"

"Let's start with your piano lesson. How did that go?"

Claire presented a report that was just-a-bit more glowing than accurate.

4

Lily smiled. Claire, she thought, you can always count on Claire.

"Will Faht be home in time for you to go to Ford's? I can go if he's too late, you know. I'd love to see *Guys and Dolls*." Without taking a breath, Claire added, "I wish that next year you'd get me tickets to go with you."

Lily nodded. She knew how Claire loved plays, the theater. "But next year you'll have graduated, and who knows what you'll be doing? So much life ahead of you."

Claire giggled. "I know. And I'm hoping – well, you know, Daniel."

Lily's mouth hardened as she negotiated the turn onto Franklin Street. She kept her eyes on the rush hour traffic. "Now you know I think Daniel is a nice boy. But, Claire, he's a boy, nowhere near to settling down. Don't forget that." She forced a smile.

"And don't you go settling down either. You are too young, too smart, too pretty, to limit your life. You could have anything, do anything, you want. Even college. I wish you'd at least consider that."

"But you weren't even eighteen when you married Faht. And Louisa. She was nineteen, barely. Why wouldn't you want that for me?"

Lily gripped the steering wheel. She blinked, hard, willing away the sudden dizziness.

Her tone sharp, she answered. "That was the war. Two wars. Those times were different. People weren't using their heads. All we thought of was – I don't know, the glamour, the romance of marrying a soldier before he went off to war, never knowing if we'd ever be together again. Like it was in a book."

Lily turned to her daughter. "But real life is different, Claire. You know that. Oh, your father and I, I wouldn't change that for the world. But you. You have a chance for more. Don't…"

5

Claire looked toward Lily, alarmed that she had stopped talking. She heard her mother moan, felt the car hit the curb, jump the pavement. Her head hit the windshield as the Packard mounted the three marble steps of the brick row house.

She screamed, "Mamma, what's wrong? What happened?"

She heard horns blaring, sensed a man opening her door. She screamed for her mother.

Tuesday

The waitress greeted August as he descended the wooden stairway, noticed that his steps were slower, more tentative these days. He held his gold-handled cane in his left hand, while his right gripped the carved banister rail.

Guten Abend, Herr Ziegler, she sang out, glad to see him, and anticipating a large tip this evening. He was more generous since the war.

"Ah, Trude, good to see you are working this evening. I'm meeting my godson, so give us a quiet table, would you?"

"He is already here, and he asked for exactly the same thing." The dirndl-clad hostess led them to a table in a dark corner of the Rathskeller. August noted Trude's legs and ankles. Swollen, he thought. Not an easy life for her. Getting old, like all of us. He resolved to give her an extra, what, dollar? Why not? he decided. Better for her than for my pocket.

August smiled as he saw Fritz, remembering the times they had spent here. Such celebrations. And their old haunt, Schellhase's on Howard Street. Graduations, birthdays, watching Fritz grow tall, to manhood. Through thick and thin as they say here, he thought. It was the thin that he knew Fritz wanted to talk about.

The factory, such high-flying days during the war. And now. Times change, August thought, and noticed that even Fritz had changed, thinner, a bit stooped, tired, a grey pallor to his skin.

August stopped leaning on his cane, pulled himself erect. If Fritz is old, what does that make me? he wondered. No. *Willenssache*. Mind over matter, as they say here.

He quickened his step. "Ah, Fritz, *mein Sohn*."

Fritz stood to pull out the chair for August, then shook his hand. "*Onkel* August," he said, giving the older man a slight bow.

The two took their places at the table. Trude, who had been standing at a respectful distance from the table, brought the two men menus. "And will you have your drinks now?"

The men nodded. Trude knew what to bring.

August opened the menu, but didn't look at it. "Let's order quickly. I sense you have something on your mind. Souse with potato salad for me."

Fritz nodded, but said nothing. August waited.

Trude delivered their drinks, and, noting August's closed menu, stood, pencil in hand. Order taken, she nodded, realizing that tonight was not the time for their usual banter.

August re-arranged the silverware at his place. Concentrating on that, he said, "Let us begin, Fritz. What is the problem? Spit it out and we can go on. Use our time well. No dilly-dally."

Fritz pulled out the gold-and-white pack of Chesterfields, tamped it on the table before he pulled out a cigarette. August watched while he flipped the top of his lighter. Stalling for time, he thought.

Fritz inhaled, smiled. "I'm stalling for time, I guess," he said, and put his head into his right hand. "*Onk*, I'm in a jam. Money. My streak of luck has run out." He looked down, took a deep drag from his cigarette.

August remained silent, and kept his face expressionless. Get on with it, Fritz, he thought.

"It's the factory. You know that it's been tough, since the end of the war, since those contracts ended. I've tried to get others to

7

replace them. But the department stores, Hutzler's, Hochschild's, I've been to them all. Hamburgers, they look to New York, to the big manufacturers. I've made arrangements to go there next week, at least to the ones who've agreed to see me. But my time is running out. I've cut back hours for the workers. Haven't had to let anyone go yet, but they see the inventories stacking up, sitting up there on the second floor. They're not stupid. But there's no place for them to go either. So it's a fuckup, to be sure.

"And that's not the biggest fuckup."

August studied his godson, surprised at the language that appeared to come so easily to him. Not like Fritz, he thought. Something beyond the factory worrying him.

August put down his beer. "Fritz, *yah*, this is bad. But we have been through bad before. The Great War, the Depression, this last war. And we are still here, drinking beer at the *Deutsches Haus*."

"No, August, this isn't the same." Fritz realized that his voice was raised. He leaned in toward his godfather. "Well, here is it. I might as well spit it all out. I mortgaged the house to keep the factory running. And that looks like it's all a cockup. If something doesn't turn around, if I don't find a way out of it, the house, the factory, it's all gone. The bank will take over; what they'll do with it, I don't know. Maybe they'll run things better than I could.

"So there you have it. A fiasco, a shambles, a failure." Fritz leaned back. "Funny, I feel almost relieved just saying it." He held his cigarette, not quite touching his lips. He shrugged. "Did you think that you'd be father-confessor this evening, *Onk*?"

August sat, deciding if it would be better to be silent, wondering if Fritz wanted advice, fearing that he might want money.

"I know this is my mess, only mine. And I am kicking myself for being such a madman to think that I could pull everything together. And the worst part, well, perhaps not the worst, but another great muddle. I haven't told Lily. She knows things are bad, but she doesn't know about the loan, the one on the factory.

And worse, she has no idea that I put a second mortgage on the house.

"So I am facing it on all fronts. I've done this all myself. There is not a soul I can blame. One bad, stupid decision after another. All because I was sure that I could pull it out, make it work.

"After all those good years, all that work, the factory humming like it never did before, I thought that I could do anything. I thought that I was the one making it work. But it was luck, a stroke of luck, the war. To profit from the war. Maybe this is my just desserts, what I get, retribution."

August reached for his godson, stopped short of his hand. "Now, Fritz, that's not so. To have the luck of getting a contract, making shirts, that is hardly profiteering. And you gave work to so many, all those women who came to you. You did good for them. So, everybody profited. That is not the same as profiteering. Put that one aside.

"You have enough to worry about, real things, without making up some story that might come from the bible. Forget that. That is feeling sorry for yourself. What you need to do is concentrate on figuring a way out, not hold your head and say that you deserve punishment. You took some risks and they didn't work out. That, my boy, is what risk is. So, this time you're on the wrong side of it.

"But changes are to come. *So leid, so leid*, but sorry doesn't fix things." August paused as Trude laid their meals before them. She knew to be quick and quiet.

August piled his fork with potato salad. The men ate in silence.

After a few minutes, Fritz looked up. "So. There you have it. A mess."

August pushed his plate to the side. "Let us look at specifics here. What is the timeframe you have? Exactly. How many weeks, I am assuming weeks, do you have? What contact have you had with the bank? Who have you talked to?"

9

An hour later, the men ended the meal with a toast, their usual, German cognac and Bernhard beer. Fritz reached for the check. August did not stop him.

"Thank you for meeting me, August. I know the time was off. And I'm off to Ellicott City; Lily and I head back downtown to Ford's this evening."

As they left the restaurant, Fritz reached to help August negotiate the stone steps to the street. August shook his head. "No help. No help needed." Though Fritz detected that his godfather was short of breath and noticed that he leaned heavily on his cane.

As the two men shook hands, August waved Fritz off as he leaned in to embrace him. "None of that, *Sohn*. None of that."

Friday

I thought I could work it out. I was going to tell you, really, I was. After it was over, after I had worked it out. I was going to tell you; you have to believe me.

Fritz placed his hand on Lily's shoulder.

I thought I could work it out, thought I could get new customers, like before. That they'd be happy to place orders, like before. And at a discount, a big discount, toward the end. When I went back to them I was practically begging. Flop sweat. I could feel it. So could they. And all the history, the shared drinks and dinners and pats-on-the-back, all that was gone. I was just a pitiful salesman to them. I had lost my edge, and they knew it.

Oh, some of them were kind. I see that now. But the days for hand-sewn shirts, well, that's over, at least in Baltimore. Maybe even New York. A new era we're in. Two of them said that – the same phrase they used, like they had been to a meeting, a convention that I missed.

Such a change from the war years. Riding high. I thought it would always be that way for us. Or maybe I didn't think at all.

This is my fault, all my fault. The factory, there's no hope for it. I was sure that I could pull this off, get us back on keel. If only I had the right contacts. I know they're out there, maybe not in Baltimore, maybe, I don't know where they could be. New York? But they have sewn it up with the big factories, the mills. Some said that they'd look to Japan. Stupid. That will never work. No one will buy anything made there.

He paused, backed away from her, sat in the chair to her left.

I was going to tell you. Really, I was.

We did get an offer, for the factory, the building. They said they'd keep the workers, if they could adapt. They said they'd let me stay for a while, if I could adapt.

That was the word they used. "Adapt." And that factory was mine, Lily, for twenty years almost. First with the shirts. Finest made. That's what Hutzler's, what Garfinkel's said, what they wanted on the labels, "fine tailoring, fine craftmanship." Remember when we got those contracts? Remember those times?

Then the war years. All those shirts – khaki, dress, whatever they wanted we could make. Our little factory getting those contracts. And the tons of fabric delivered – they thought about running a rail spur right to the back door. Remember that? And running two shifts, then seven days, then three shifts – and all the workers happy. Everyone making money. More orders, like they'd never stop. The trucks in and out, the Army widening Fels Lane to accommodate them.

And the house on the hill. A dream, your dream. The big house, dogwood trees lining the drive. "A cloud of pink" you called it, remember? And I, well, I was going to be a gentleman farmer. Such days, such dreams for us, Lily.

Fritz leaned forward, rested his arms on his knees.

I was going to tell you. I was. And now, no need. So it was good that you died not knowing. Not good that you died, but good that you didn't know, that I hadn't told you.

What I might get from the bank, not enough to recover the money I'd spent on the up-fit. All that equipment I bought, useless now. And the house as collateral. They called in the loan. And so that is gone, or will be, too. I never had to tell you that.

I haven't told the girls. I will. I'll have to. Soon. I couldn't tell them now. Not yet.

He placed his hand atop Lily's. She would not have wanted to be buried in that dress, that much he knew. Louisa must have been so upset when she chose it that she didn't realize. One of Lily's work dresses, it still had a smear of carbon paper on the cuff. And something else. Her face. Something was off, though he couldn't quite identify it.

As he stared at his wife's body, he realized. The lipstick, a dark purple, not a good choice for a corpse. Lily didn't look like herself.

And her rings, the diamond that she always wore, the one he'd given her when they got that first big contract. Where were they?

He'd ask Louisa about that. Thank god for Louisa, taking care of everything.

He bent down and studied her body. His Lily, yet not, not quite, the skin too white, cheeks too pink, her lips too dark. He kissed her, once on the forehead, once on the mouth, then stepped back to the chair, put his head in his hands.

Lily gone. A nightmare. Thank god for Louisa. He exhaled and looked straight ahead. She'll take care of everything.

Two

Claire stood in the doorway, watching her father. Since Lily's death, she felt odd about entering the room that heretofore she had bounded into each morning, always checking the hem of her blue serge uniform jumper in the full-length mirror that hung on the door of her mother's closet. Now the room had taken on another dimension; it was different without Lily.

Fritz looked up. He too felt the change in the house. Anticipation, he thought. The house is waiting for Lily to come home, to turn on her purple Crosley radio, always tuned to WBAL, *The Breakfast Club*, her soap operas, *Aunt Jenny's Real-Life Stories*. He missed teasing her about them. He missed hearing her hum "Blue Skies," always in that tone that was a bit flat. It irritated him when he was cross with her; it enchanted him when he was not.

Lily, always Lily. Their ups and downs, the downs so desolate, the ups he could never quite trust to last. But their last days had been good. He was relieved that he had delayed telling her, disclosing, exposing, the impending catastrophe. He had put it off, wanting to give it one more week, one more try. And then. Well, now he didn't have to tell her.

But soon he would have to say something to the girls, not the whole story, perhaps, but something that they could understand.

Fritz moved to the window, put his hand on the desk that stood in that corner of the room. Lily's. Lily's desk. He turned to Claire, motioned for her to enter.

"She kept our baby books here, in the bottom drawer," Claire said, bending to touch the mahogany. "And her note paper, her note cards in the middle drawer. Sometimes I would come in when she was out and go through them.

Sneaky, I guess." Claire's last words were lost in a shaky sob.

Fritz put his arm around her. "We're all like that, wanting to know what others think, what they do when they're not with us. Too much Nancy Drew for you, do you think?"

Claire shifted away, wiped her eyes with her left hand. "Well, much too old for Nancy Drew now." She smiled.

Fritz squared his shoulders. "Mr. Summers has asked for your mother's will. Just a technicality. I thought it would be in the safe deposit box, but I didn't find it there. Come, help me go through her things here."

He stopped. "That is, if you think you're up to it, if it won't upset you." He remembered his tears when he saw his wife's handwriting on a note to him, reminding him to pick up dog food. The small things, he thought, those are the things that stop you cold.

Claire hesitated. "I'd like that, Faht. I'd like to help you, be with you when you do this."

Both were silent and dry-eyed as they pulled long-forgotten notes and scribblings from the pigeon-holed desk, reminders of massage appointments, lunch dates, Mothers' Club meetings, ticket stubs from Ford's Theatre, movie stubs from The Century, the Mayfair.

Fritz pulled two envelopes from the top drawer. The first, a copy of the will. He opened it. All seemed in order, and he briefly wondered why she had taken it from the bank. He saw his name, Lily's handwriting, on the envelope behind it. The rubber band that held them together snapped in his hand. Old, brittle, like I feel today, he thought.

He put the envelopes in the breast pocket of his jacket. He was to meet with Summers the next day and take care of …

14

what, he thought. Fritz tried to picture what Lily's death would mean, what difference her will would make. They had given all they had to each other. Now neither had anything to give.

Claire was the first to notice the manila folder at the bottom of the drawer. She looked to her father before she touched it. Handing it to Fritz, she waited. Being with her father, sharing this task, taking on an adult role, his assistant, even his confidante, gave her an unexpected feeling of adulthood. Maybe I can really help him, she thought. She noted the puzzled look on her father's face, waited for him to speak.

Fritz opened the folder, read the documents contained in it. "This is yours, Claire. From your mother. It's an insurance policy, made out to you." He looked at the pages in the file. "She took it out when we bought this house."

He riffled the pages of the policy, then looked at the now empty drawer. "I wonder why there isn't one for Louisa? We must look for it."

He handed the file to Claire, while he knelt to go through the drawers once again. Finding nothing, he pulled the small drawers on the desktop, put his fingers in all the pigeon holes to make sure that he had not overlooked it. Claire watched, saying nothing.

When he was sure that there was no policy to be found, he turned to his younger daughter. "Best to say nothing to Louisa about this. Let's keep looking. I'm sure your mother would not have had only one, never one for you and not your sister." He stood by the desk and said nothing. Claire watched, aware of the ticking of the clock by the bed.

When she could stand it no longer, she said, "Should I keep this then? Do you want me to keep it, or do you want it?"

Fritz started; he had forgotten his younger daughter was there. "No, you keep it. We'll sort things out later." He turned, put his arm around her. "You've not had an easy time of it, have you? You keep that policy. I'll talk to Summers about it. It might be just what you need."

A few weeks later, Claire was setting the table in the kitchen. Nettie had left a pot simmering on the back of the stove. It's nice to have this time, me and Faht, she thought. She knew how little time, how few meals they had shared since her mother's death, the two of them at home. Most times either Louisa was there, or they went to her house, or they ate out, Chinese, Uncle Lee's, on Garrison Boulevard, where she and Fritz and Lily often ate on their way back from downtown. Always the same – pork egg rolls, pork fried rice, shrimp egg foo yung. When the waiters asked about Lily, why she wasn't with them, Claire saw her father's throat clench. He told them, they embarrassed that they had caused him to be embarrassed. So hard, all these things, telling people who didn't know, then comforting them in their discomfort.

Sniffing back her tears, she saw that Fritz had pulled the car into the garage. Good, she thought, he's home for the night. We'll have some time together.

He came in through the kitchen door, smiled at his daughter. Lovely that she's doing this, trying to make things normal for us, he thought. Like it was before. Then he remembered. It will never be like it was before, Lily's place at the table empty now. These realizations come like electric shocks, he thought.

"Give me a minute to wash up, then we'll have an early dinner, maybe read some after. What are you reading these days?" Fritz asked.

"Just homework, homework, homework. I could bring it down and do it in the living room. That way we could be together." She hesitated. "And there is something that I maybe could talk to you about?" Her inflection rose on her last words.

Fritz stopped as he placed his hat on the rack behind the door to the back stairway. "Something important, Claire? We could talk about it now if you want."

"Maybe after dinner. How about that?"

Fritz nodded and ascended the stairs. Once in his room, he threw his jacket onto the bed. General was stretched out on Lily's side, the German Shepherd taking up the majority of the place where his wife once laid. "Don't bother getting up, General. Glad that somebody's getting some sleep in this room."

He went into the bathroom, washed his face and hands, looked into the mirror. No one would know what trouble you're in, buddy. I guess that's good. Flop sweat not readily apparent. That phrase is never far from me, he thought. Let me hide it from Claire, for now, at least. He double-cuffed the sleeves of his shirt and returned to the kitchen.

"Smelling good. Nettie's doing a good job, and you're doing a great job keeping the house going."

Claire spooned the stew into bowls. "Well, Louisa stops in a lot. I don't think that Nettie is too happy about that." Claire put the bowls on the table. "Maybe you could mention something to her, let her know that she really doesn't have to check up. I think Nettie feels that's what Louisa's doing, and you know how Louisa can be sometimes."

Fritz went to the refrigerator, removed a bottle of Lowenbrau, brought it back to the table, something, he remembered, that Lily would not have allowed. "At least put it in a glass, Fritz." Her voice sounded so real, so close, that Fritz closed his eyes.

Claire noticed. "Are you okay, Faht?"

Fritz nodded, then smiled. "So, let's talk about what you have to talk about. Then we can talk some more after dinner, if you'd like."

Claire smiled. This would go just fine. Faht will understand. He'll tell me what to do. She took a deep breath, took a bite of potato and began:

"Well, Sister Cleodes asked me to come to her office today. She pulled me out of class. I thought that it was something about Mamma. Why else would she have wanted to see me? But it was about something entirely different. She asked me about college, if I had given any thought to college.

"I didn't know what to say. I haven't thought about anything except Mamma since, well, you know, since the accident. But I didn't want her to know that. I didn't know what to say. And I guess she is right. I should be thinking about next year. I was going to do that, we all were, all the girls. But then we got so caught up with, you know, the holidays, and parties. And then, well, you know.

"So I used Mamma as an excuse. I felt terrible, but I couldn't think of anything to say, and I felt so stupid because I hadn't any plans.

"But she didn't seem to even notice that. She wanted to talk about college, colleges really, that she thought would be good for me. And they were away, away from Baltimore. Well, she did mention Notre Dame, but that was just a mention. The ones she talked about were in Philadelphia, New York, I think, and then one in Washington. She said that they were all good Catholic schools and that I would be looked after there, and, most of all, get an education that I deserved. That's the term she used, 'deserved'."

Claire watched her father as she spoke. He pulled a wedge of bread from the loaf and dipped it into the stew's gravy. He held it in his left hand as he considered his response.

"College," he said. Measuring his words, he continued, "You have your mother's insurance money. You could use it for that, for college. There's enough, you wouldn't have to worry about money for tuition." And neither would I, he thought. "But I never thought about your going away from home. There are colleges right here; you could go to school, like you're doing now. Even Strayer's Business College downtown, if you'd be interested in that."

He paused before he spoke. "But college, away from home, living on campus, that could give you a real experience, one that none of us had." He warmed to the subject. "And if you could do that, don't limit yourself to what the nuns suggest. Branch out a bit, a lot; get out from under those Catholic wings, get a chance to experience the world."

Fritz leaned back, looked at his daughter. "You know, with all that's happened, I never gave it a thought, Claire. But if you think that's something you'd like, let's look at some schools for you."

"But what about you? What would you do here, all by yourself?"

Fritz reached across the table, took Claire's hand. "I see tears, there. No more tears. We've all shed enough. You've shed more than any teenager needs to shed. I'll be just fine. And it's not like you're moving away. It would be like you were at boarding school, learning new things, meeting new people. Really, Claire, this could open up so many avenues for you. Think about it."

Fritz was surprised at his enthusiasm for his daughter's opportunity. Why hadn't I thought of it before? Claire, always sweet, never any trouble, so easy to forget about, with all that swirled about them.

He resolved to talk to August, get his thoughts on things. Claire's voice interrupted his thoughts.

"Faht, do you think I should talk to Daniel about it? See what he thinks? See if he thinks I should go away. Maybe he would want me here, to be with him when he's in school."

Hearing this, Fritz put his bottle down on the table, a bit harder than he intended.

"Claire, I wouldn't get too involved, as young as you are. I know that your mother and I married young, that Louisa did, but the circumstances were different. War makes people not think straight. But times are different now. You have opportunities that we never dreamed of.

"I think you should consider college. Yes. Let's see if we can meet with August, get his thoughts. We could make a celebration of it."

Fritz stood, took his plate to the sink, scraped the remains into the garbage bin. Nettie would take care of things when she arrived the next morning. He turned to Claire.

"It might be best not to say anything to Louisa. Not yet. Not until we have things a bit more sorted out."

Claire nodded, relieved. Somehow when Louisa was involved, things became knotty.

Nettie rolled her eyes as Louisa positioned herself at the kitchen table. Claire had just arrived home from school, her textbooks still in her arms. Louisa pointed to the table, indicated that Claire should sit. Claire sat.

It's as if I'm invisible, Nettie thought, and walked into the pantry where she could hear and continue not to be seen.

"You stay with us. It will be better that way. You won't be in Faht's way. He won't have to worry about you. You can babysit Charlotte. I'll help him with the business and getting rid of this house. Good riddance. He never wanted it anyway. It was her idea, all her, always what she wanted. Never, she never gave a thought to him what would be best for him. Selfish. That's all she was."

Louisa's face flushed scarlet. Claire watched her older sister, chewed on her lower lip. She had been on the receiving end of these diatribes for as long as she could remember. At least you've stopped beating me, she thought, and was grateful for that. Twelve years separating the two, Claire was never a match for her.

Louisa's voice rose. "You sit there saying nothing, doing nothing. Like the stupid stick you are. A brat, a spoiled brat. Just doing anything she said, anything she wanted, trying to make her love you. She didn't, you know. She thought you were stupid. She knew you were stupid. Spineless. That's what she called you.

"Oh yes, she would call me to talk about you. Stupid, weak, spineless, and ugly on top of it. A nothing – that's the term she used. She said it over and over. 'Claire, she's a nothing. She will never amount to anything. A blob, don't you think?'

"That's what she'd say, and then laugh. We both would laugh. Because that's what you are. A joke, nothing but a joke."

Louisa got up from her chair, came close to Claire, her face inches away.

"And you sit there. You don't have a word to say for yourself. That's because you know it's true, don't you? You know that you are nothing."

Claire pushed her chair back from the kitchen table, moved to get around her older sister, headed for the back stairway. Louisa ran to block her way. Claire turned away, fought to keep her composure. She turned sideways to get by Louisa. "Leave me alone," she screamed, hearing a sob come from her throat. "Why do you always do this? Why do you hate me so much?"

Louisa, calm now, the color gone from her face, smiled.

"Why are you so upset? Why would you think that I hate you?" She paused, picked up the car keys that she had laid by the sink. "The only person who hates you is yourself."

Her expression changed, softened. She smiled as she turned to face Claire. "So, pack a bag for a couple of weeks, at least. I'll ask Charles to pick you up after dinner. Now I've told Faht that coming to stay with us is your idea, that there are too many sad memories here for you. So you make sure that's the only story he hears. If you love him, you won't want to worry him.

"I don't want him to worry. Do you understand me?" Louisa locked her eyes onto Claire's.

Claire nodded, turned, and walked up the stairs to her room. She pulled the tan Lady Baltimore suitcases, a present for her sixteenth birthday, out from under the bed.

Nettie returned to the kitchen. White people, she thought, making their own hell.

Three

The trees were in full leaf as Claire hurried down the street, catching herself as she tripped on the sidewalk lifted by hundred-year-old roots. She knew Louisa would be ready to leave as soon as she walked in the door. Charlotte would be hungry, grumpy and wanting to be fed. The five-year-old always calmed down after her mother left. Claire knew that and was ready for her.

Louisa wasn't standing at the door as she usually was. Claire wondered about that, but thought that she had mislaid her car keys again. As she let herself in the house, Louisa called to her from the kitchen. "I've got something for you to see. I sent away for them and they just arrived in the morning's mail."

Claire smiled. Louisa had thought of her. She threw her books on the damask sofa before heading to the kitchen.

"Look at these. I thought you could study them while I'm out. We can talk when I get home." She shoved the large envelopes toward Claire. "Go ahead, open them."

Claire looked up at Louisa "They're from the WAVEs, the WACs."

"Go ahead." Louisa brushed her auburn hair back from her face. "Open them. I can't wait with you forever. I've got to leave."

Claire spread the pamphlets on the kitchen table. Charlotte came into the room and pushed up against her. Claire turned to kiss the child on the head.

"You can do all that later, Claire. Look at these pamphlets. I sent away for them for you. I think this is what you need. Join the service. They'll take care of you, make sure you have a job, somewhere to live. You can travel. You can do all sorts of things. And you get a month's vacation every year so you can travel wherever you'd like. It is a great opportunity. All you have to do is fill out these forms. I'll take them to the recruitment office for you. Then they'll call and it will be all set." Louisa's voice was excited. Charlotte looked at her mother, puzzled by her exhilaration.

Claire put her hand on the red-white-and-blue brochures, each picturing a well-groomed woman in uniform. Very attractive women, she thought, then turned to Louisa. "I don't understand. What are these for? What do you want me to do with them?"

Louisa threw a scarlet cashmere cardigan across her shoulders. "I don't have time to talk about it now. Look them over while I'm gone. We'll talk when I get back. But I think it is the perfect plan for your future. You'll graduate soon. It doesn't look like you've given any thought to your future. This is the best thing for you. Provide you with stability. I think you need that. You can't expect Faht to take care of you. He has enough worries. You certainly don't want to be a burden to him. This is the perfect answer. You'll be taken care of, and he won't have to worry, think about you.

Louisa saw Claire's hesitation. She stared at her sister. "Don't you think he has enough on his mind? You want to add to that?"

Claire swallowed, closed her eyes, hoping it would help the dizziness. She felt her head spinning. She tried to speak, tried to respond in a way that wouldn't add to Louisa's fury.

"Louisa, no, no, I don't want to be a burden. I don't. But I don't know, maybe he doesn't want to be left alone. Maybe it would be a good thing if I moved back with him, helped him get over Mamma's death. I don't know if I'm ready to go out on my own either. It seems so sudden."

"Well, you don't have to worry about his being alone. I'm here. It's just if you were taken care of, the Army, or the Navy, then he wouldn't have to worry about you." Louisa's eyes, her tone, were soft, caring. Claire watched her sister's mood change. She knew enough not to trust it.

Louisa moved closer. "It seems to me that you're being pretty selfish, thinking only of yourself. After all, you wouldn't be here to take care of Charlotte, and I'm willing to sacrifice that. Just to see that you are on your way in the world.

"Plus, this is an opportunity for you. You don't want to be stuck in a life like mine. Really, if someone had presented such a prospect to me, I would have thanked them, not put up such a fuss."

Claire opened her mouth, willed herself to speak. "I'm not putting up a..."

Louisa interrupted her sister. "This would give you a chance to do something with your life, to see the world."

"But, Louisa, I do want a life like yours. You have it all – a house, a husband, a child. Who wouldn't want that? That's what I want for Daniel and me. What you have. That's what all my friends want. To be married. How could I go away and leave Daniel? Why would I do that?"

Louisa threw down her sweater. "Daniel? You think Daniel wants to marry you? God, you are a child, and a stupid one at that."

She turned toward the door. "I have to leave. I cannot believe that you are acting like this."

Charlotte pulled on Claire's skirt. "Mommy's angry. Don't make her mad."

Claire followed her sister to the front door. "Louisa, don't be angry. Really, thank you. It's just so sudden. And to leave home. I don't know how to think about it. I assumed..."

"That's just like you, isn't it? You assume. You assume that everything will work out like you want it, that everyone will be there for you." Louisa's face flushed. "Well, you better get over it. Your mother's not here to protect you now. You're on your own. So now you better take what's offered and be glad of it."

"Louisa, she was our mother." Claire stopped, swallowed. "Don't go like this. Stay a minute so we can talk."

Louisa closed the door without turning back.

Charlotte pulled on Claire's arm. "Mommy's mad. You better watch out."

Claire turned toward her niece. "Come sit on my lap. Then we'll fix some spaghetti. Out of the can. Just like you like it."

25

She rested her chin on Charlotte's head. Daniel, she thought. Daniel. We could get married. I could get a job while he finished school. That would work. That would make everything all right

The next week, a visit home for Claire at Sylvan Cliffs. She cleared the dishes, then placed them in the sink to soak. Fritz stayed at the dining room table.

He's distracted, she thought, or grieving, or tired. Now is not the time to add to his burdens. So then, when? He's here, but not here. Never here. Never.

She straightened her shoulders and returned to the dining room. "Faht."

Fritz looked up.

"Do you have a minute. It won't take long. There's something I have to ask you, something I need to figure out."

Fritz shifted in his chair, patted the seat next to him. "Here, sit, Lily's chair."

Since her death, Fritz and Claire had shifted from their usual places; Lily's chair had remained empty.

Claire hesitated, then pulled the chair from the table, and sat down, straightening her blue uniform skirt. She felt her heart race and knew it was as much from what she wanted to say as from occupying the chair that had been her mother's.

Fritz watched her. "Another milestone, Claire. To remember, not enshrine."

Claire let out a breath she hadn't realized that she'd held. She felt her eyes fill, willed herself not to cry. She could do that later, for as long as she liked. She folded her hands in her lap, looked down at the table, traced the lace patterns in the tablecloth.

"Faht, it's Louisa."

Fritz sighed. "Oh, Claire, let's not revisit this. That's just how she is. She doesn't mean anything by it." He stopped himself, reached to touch Claire's shoulder. "Oh, sorry, sorry." Fritz sighed. "What has she done now?"

Claire debated with herself whether to continue or be quiet. She bit her lip. Silent, once again silent, she thought.

"I don't know what to tell you, Claire. She's always been, well, you know, with your mother, with you. Lily said, you remember, she said it a lot. 'Sisters just don't get along. All sisters argue. Mothers and daughters don't get along. Then everything turns out.'

"Why do you let it affect you? You should ignore her when she gets like that. That's all. You have to ignore her."

"Faht, how can you say that?" Claire felt her face flush. "I've tried ignoring her, tried your advice, Mamma's advice. It may work for you, but when I do it, she gets more and more vicious, more hateful. You know that. You've seen it. You always excuse her. She knows it and it makes her even more..."

Fritz pushed back his chair. One more thing, one more god-damned thing, he thought. How much more? Everything collapsing. "I don't know what to tell you, Claire. She means well, she really does."

Claire stood up; she felt her knees shake. Her throat tightened. She heard her words come out as a squeak. "How can you say that, Faht. How can you let her do, say, anything to me, anything she pleases? You've always made excuses for her, for the beatings. You've always done that. Don't I count for anything? Don't I count at all?"

"Claire, sit down. There's no use..." Fritz stopped, exhaled. "Just try to work it out yourselves. You have Lily's money now. I told you to keep it, that it belongs to you. I took up for you there. I don't always defend Louisa. It is not fair of you to say that, and I certainly don't want you to think it."

Fritz thought of Lily's letter to him, the one he found tucked behind her will. It told of the insurance policy she had bought for Claire, Claire, whom she described as "the quiet breath in the corner of life, never causing any trouble." The money, Lily wrote, would be an ounce of recognition, of understanding that we had always taken her love, her presence, for granted.

He turned to face Claire, shook his head. "Let's forget this for now. You know I love you; I love you both." Fritz rested his head in his right hand.

"This is not about love, Faht, really it isn't."

Fritz pushed his chair back, stood. "Enough, Claire. Don't do this to me."

Claire watched her father leave the room. Fritz walked to his study and closed the door, harder than he had intended. She slept in her old room that night, and returned to Louisa's the next morning.

Later in that week, she waited until Louisa and Charles had gone upstairs for the evening. They nodded when Claire told them that she would close up the downstairs for the evening. She had already tucked Charlotte in for the night.

She heard Charles walk to his daughter's room. Claire knew he checked in on her every night before he went to his room. She listened for the click of their door, waited, counting three minutes, and went to the phone in the hallway niche.

Fritz picked up on the third ring. A late call, he thought, never bodes well. He was relieved, and then concerned, when he heard Claire's voice.

She started talking before he had a chance to speak.

"I'm so sorry to call this late, Faht, but I had to talk to you. I don't want to worry you. Everything is fine. Really. But I miss you, miss my home. I know you have a lot of worries now, but could I see you? Tomorrow? I'll get the bus so you won't have to come get me.

Fritz offered to pick her up at Louisa's. "We can have lunch at Marty Welch's like we used to do. Saturday lunch, remember that? Maybe Louisa can come with us. Like the old times."

Except, Claire did not point out, that it had been the three of them, Claire, Fritz, and Lily. Louisa had never been part of the group.

Claire kept her voice low. "Oh, Faht, I want to come home. I won't be a bother, I promise. I miss you, miss Sylvan Cliffs so much. I feel that everything I know, everything I've ever loved..." Claire stopped, swallowed hard.

"I'll get the streetcar to Main Street. You don't need to pick me up. Would that be all right? Around noon? I can stop at the bakery for buns. Like we used to have. From Leidig's."

Fritz sighed. "Claire, this is your home. You don't have to ask permission to come home. Ever. Why would you think that? I'll come to Louisa's tomorrow morning. I'll come get you."

Claire interrupted him. "No, Faht. Don't do that. I'll take the bus. I'll tell Louisa I'm meeting my girlfriends downtown. Please don't say anything to her that I'm coming. Please. Promise."

Fritz rubbed his right eyebrow. "Claire, what's wrong? Do I need to come and get you tonight? Has Louisa done something? I thought you wanted to go to Louisa's, stay there, with Charlotte, that Sylvan Cliffs held too many sad memories of your mother. What happened? Tell me."

Claire recognized the alarm in her father's voice. "No, no. Nothing bad. I just...," her voice broke, "miss you." She swallowed hard, stood straight. "Really, nothing's wrong. I feel better talking to you.

Claire drew her shoulders back, took in a deep breath. "I'll see you tomorrow. And I'll bring buns." She tried to laugh. "I love you, Daddy."

Fritz closed his eyes. "And I love you too, my Clairedelune."

He heard Claire replace the receiver. My little girl, he thought, maybe I shouldn't have let her to move to Louisa's. Her last time at home, her last time here at Sylvan Cliffs. Maybe she needs to be here, with me, with Lily.

And that Sunday Claire moved back, to Sylvan Cliffs, to Fritz, and Nettie, and to her beloved General.

Four

Fritz dressed carefully that morning. He wanted to look his best, for them. His life, eventually, he believed, would get back on track; for his workers, he wasn't so sure. The buyers said they would keep the staff on. Fritz wanted to believe that, but didn't.

He noticed the few cars, rusted, that sat by the wooden railing at the lot's edge. Most of the workers walked from the mill town of Oella that hugged the east side of the Tiber River. Fritz sat behind the wheel, thinking about them. His workers and their families had lived here for more than a hundred years. The woolen mills ran steadily during the war, but it was the shirt factory, his shirt factory, and the nearby doughnut mill, converted to manufacturing weaponry, that were the stars of the town. The sweet smell of sugary doughnuts being baked was missed, but the residents enjoyed the influx of money being spent.

Fritz's business was smaller, not a big player, tucked away off Main Street on Fels Lane. But the word soon got out that it was a good place to work, cleaner than most, less dust, lint, than the mills. Not as much money as the weapons plant, but some liked the idea of working smaller, without the constant clangor of metal tooling. Not as much chance of being blown up, as some of the men sniggered.

Fritz thought about his employees from lower Fels Lane, that small Negro community. None worked the machines, but they were glad to get jobs cleaning. None of the other mills employed any Negro workers. He wondered, despite the promises of the new owners, how they would fare.

The employees admired Fritz. Some, the women, fantasized that he would sweep them off their feet, take them to live in New York City, a location so far removed from their circumstances that they knew all they could do was dream. Lily knew this as well, and so made sure that her presence was known, and felt, when she came in two, sometimes three, days a week to "keep the books," as she said. She took care to smile when she walked to the office at the back of the first floor, sure that her make-up was fresh, no dark roots apparent.

Claire visited frequently, always bringing a sweet that she had baked. The employees agreed that her efforts were almost inedible, but praised her anyway. Worth it to see her smile, they said. Once she brought Charlotte with her, but the child cried and asked to go home. No, Fritz, and Claire, those were the ones the workers liked.

Fritz forced himself to leave the car, straightened his shoulders, and strode toward the entrance. Do this for them, he thought. Give them hope; give them courage. He swallowed and smiled as he pulled open the black enameled door.

The night watchman, a black man possessing few teeth and a wisdom that belied his station in life, greeted him. "Good to see you early this morning, Mr. Fritz. How's my Miss Claire doing at her fancy school?"

Fritz clapped him on the shoulder. "She's doin' fine, Dick. She always asks about you. Wants to be sure that you save your cigar boxes for her." Dick was Claire's favorite at the factory. He smoked King Edward Imperials cigars. A corner of her desk at Sylvan Cliffs contained stacks of his cigar boxes, filled with letters, ticket stubs, old photographs, that made that part of her room smell faintly of cheap tobacco.

Dick waited. He, and the rest of the staff, knew that something was brewing. Fritz away from the plant so often, inventories spilling beyond the shelves.

"Would you ask everyone to meet me in the cutting rooms. They can put their machines on idle. This won't take long." This feels as grim as Lily's funeral, Fritz thought, then turned and walked smartly to the back of the factory.

It took less than five minutes for him to say what he had to say. It came as no surprise to anyone; the only surprise was that the new owners agreed to keep them on for at least a month, and those who could "adapt," yes, Fritz used that word, would be offered a more permanent position. He added that he would stay through the first month, to introduce everyone and help to smooth the transition.

"We are seeing a new day, new challenges, new ways of doing things. Young people coming in, coming in over us," he said. "But we can adapt, we can learn, and we can show these new fellows that we know a thing or two as well. You have put in a tremendous effort. You made this company what it is, what it was. And I know that you can prove yourselves in short order.

"You have my thanks and friendship."

Fritz stopped, unsure of what to do, where to go. The employees stood, also hesitant of their next move. He heard a lone clap from the middle of the group that was soon taken up by all present. He swallowed and moved into the group, shaking hands. "I'll still be here for a while. This isn't a funeral, you know." He stopped, realized what he had just said. "Ah, that...." He shook his head, turned, and walked to his office. His employees, quiet, returned to their stations. Their conversations would wait until his car pulled out of the parking lot.

Five

Fritz didn't believe in lucky stars, though he breathed a sigh of relief and gave a brief nod to a prayer of thanksgiving. Sylvan Cliffs sold in a month, and the new owners were interested in any furniture he chose to leave. Like Lily and I, Fritz thought, when we were aglow in the happiness of moving up, showing the world our success without having to shout it. Well, I wish you better luck.

Lily's house this was, he thought, as he walked a last time through every room. He pictured her, joyful, the first time they had visited, the poplar floors, though that had to be pointed out to them, the brass hardware, window sills deep enough to sit in, now with cushions each a different, but coordinated, chintz. Lily's work. Her choice of colors, each room different, but somehow each blending into the next. She loved having the house, that she did, Fritz thought. It showed. People felt it, a house that was loved. Fritz felt it, Claire as well.

Even Nettie. Fritz had talked to the new owners about her, and they seemed grateful to have her as a resource. Nettie, Fritz thought, she'll make do. She'll definitely make do. He smiled. Another well of wisdom he'd have to leave behind.

And Louisa, she definitely did not love Sylvan Cliffs and was anything but quiet about it. Fritz turned, fingered the window. Perhaps because she had already married before they moved, had never felt at home here. Oh, Louisa. Fritz sighed. What will become of you?

He walked to the second floor, down the hallway to Claire's bedroom. Standing at the window, he touched the glass. Original sand glass the realtor told them. It was Claire who found it, calling him and Lily to come quick. "1865 Martha" scratched into the pane's lower right-hand corner. "I think she was left-handed, don't you? To write it there? Left-handed, just like me. I think I'll write '1943 Claire.' The year we moved here. That way there will be a thread." His sweet, dear daughter, so happy, untroubled then. The three of them in the house.

He heard Lily's laugh. "You will do no such thing," she said, and took Claire's hand, kissed it, and gently bit down on one of her daughter's fingers.

He would take much of the furniture in Claire's bedroom, though the bed that little Charlotte slept in would stay, as would the furniture in the dining room, the study, the sun porches and the guest bedrooms. Fritz would take his books, his bed, his favorite reading chair, plus a few odd pieces. They would fit in his apartment on University Parkway.

He had no wish to continue his conversations with Louisa about the apartment's second bedroom, Claire's, a place for Claire to call home.

He replayed Louisa's words: "Oh, Faht, you really don't think she'll want to come home, come back here. She's told me she has absolutely no plans, no desire to live in Baltimore. She loves New England. I'm sure that's where she'll stay. At least that's what she's told me. She probably hasn't said anything to you because she doesn't want to hurt your feelings.

"But, really, you need to make that room your study, your library. I can fix it up for you so that you think you're back in Ellicott City. Let me do that. Don't mess it up because you think Claire needs a place to stay. If she comes to visit, she can stay with us. You know how much Charlotte would like that."

Fritz hadn't argued with his daughter. But he tagged Claire's bed and bureau to go with the movers.

Claire had chosen Mt. Holyoke College. The nuns would have preferred a Catholic school; Fritz convinced her otherwise. "Look far, look wide, Claire. This is your chance and we are all cheering you on. You're smart; you've got a good head on your shoulders; you don't need to keep your world small."

In the spring, the two of them sat together in Fritz's study at Sylvan Cliffs and looked over brochures. She chose Mt. Holyoke because of the photos of the iron-gated entrance and the giant azaleas flanking the administration building. To her, it looked like a place where she might belong. Fritz smiled as he signed her application and wondered what Lily would have thought. Their little girl heading to Massachusetts, on her own.

That September, they drove to Union Station, and he kissed her goodbye. She hadn't visited the campus; this would be her first glimpse of Mt. Holyoke, of New England. He pressed a ten-dollar bill into her hand. The new owners had kept him on at the factory, an unexpected, albeit opportune, surprise, and he felt that he couldn't take time off to accompany her. Louisa was not present, had not emerged from her fury at learning of Lily's insurance policy.

Fritz had decided that it would be better if he be the one to tell her, at a time when Claire wasn't there. Louisa stormed, raged, lashed out at both Lily and Claire. In short order, she demanded to see the policy document. "Who sold her this? I will get in touch with him to make sure that there isn't one for me, that you are not keeping my money from me.

"All I have done for you, and this is the way that you betray me. Allowing her, that twit, that sniveling twit, to have money that she doesn't deserve. Allowing her to go to college. Allowing her to have, to do, anything she wants, when I'm the one who cares about you. She doesn't love you. She loved Lily, but she certainly doesn't care about you. All she wants to do is use you, and you can't see it."

Fritz watched his daughter, unsure when, or how, to stop her. He had seen her like this before, but it had always been about Lily. Louisa and Lily, oil and water. They had been at loggerheads since Louisa's birth. "That's how it is with mothers and daughters," Lily said, and Louisa's diatribes, harangues, attacks never seemed to affect her. Fritz remembered that slight, almost Gallic, shrug of the shoulders. Lily, why aren't you here to handle this?

Facing his older daughter, he said, "You are out of line with this, Louisa. I will not allow you to defame your mother or to attack your sister. You have had every opportunity, more in fact, than she has had. You chose to marry. You chose your life. Because she chooses a different path is no reason to strike out like this.

"It was I who made the decision to allow Claire to keep her inheritance, the insurance money, from Lily. I don't have the financial resources, if you must know, that we had when you were her age. You had everything you wanted. Don't begrudge your sister. It is unbecoming to you. She loves you; I love you. You have a family; you have a good life. Don't resent your sister's entry into the world. She has lost her mother, and I think that has affected her more deeply than it has you. It wouldn't hurt you to show her a little love."

"And it wouldn't have hurt Lily to show me a little insurance policy, would it? And it wouldn't have hurt Claire to give me half of her money, would it? How about that for your band of angels?"

Fritz stepped back. "It was I who advised Claire to keep the entire amount for her future. She suggested sharing it with you. But you have Charles, you have more than enough money. Your life is set. Hers is not. And I don't think it inappropriate that she have a bit of a nest egg, a safety net.

"This conversation is over, Louisa. I advise you to think about what we have discussed and look at your life and all that you have. Jealousy, bitterness, does not become you."

He closed his eyes as Louisa stormed out. She left her purse behind. When she came back for it, she collapsed, sobbing, into Fritz's arms.

He patted her on the back. "It will be all right, Louisa. Don't worry. It will be all right." An hour later, she called him to let him know she had arrived home safely.

And so, on this day, as he left Sylvan Cliffs for the last time, Fritz knew he would keep a room for Claire, for now at least. It would all work out with Louisa and Claire, he thought. It will all work out. Even General, the beloved German Shepherd. Dick would take General. He'd live at the factory, Dick said. And then go home with him when his shift was over. "He'll be company for us, and something to remember you and Miss Claire by."

Fritz found a parking spot close to the entrance to the Ambassador Apartments, and gave a superstitious tap to the steering wheel to bring good fortune. I can use some, he thought, in spades.

The next morning, Fritz woke before dawn. As he made a pot of coffee, no more Nettie doing this, he thought. He stood, concentrating on the sounds as the percolator did its task. So much quiet in this house, this apartment, he corrected himself, then cleared his throat. Get used to it, pal, he told himself. Get used to it.

He filled a cup to the brim and moved to his desk, which sat in a corner of the east-facing living room. Claire, he thought, a letter to Claire, to tell her.

Dearest Clairedelune,

Well, it has happened. Sylvan Cliffs has been sold. I hope that the new folks love it like you and your mother. I think it was most special to you two. And we have our memories of our years here. Really, it was the three of us, wasn't it? Such good times. The new people asked about Nettie, and I think she'll be taken care of. That is a relief. I can't imagine that kitchen without her stirring something on the stove. When I told her she hmphed, you know, like she does. But I think she was relieved. I think she'd like it if you visited her when you come back for a visit.

It feels odd to write to you like this. But there is so much that I want to say, so that you have a record of it. Of how happy you made the years here, of how happy you made your mother and me. And how proud we both are that you are taking this bold step. Off to college; off to New England, all on your own.

So, while we may not have Sylvan Cliffs anymore, you still will have your room at my new place, our new place. It's on University Parkway, across the street from Johns Hopkins. So if you and your beau are still seeing one another, he can come right across the street. I've taken the furniture from your room and will make it like home for you.

My dear Clairedelune, be brave, be smart, and know that I love you,

Faht

Claire had anticipated this letter, and after reading it, folded it and tucked it inside her journal. She memorized every word. Sylvan Cliffs gone to them. She thought of Fritz, of Lily, of Sylvan Cliffs, closed her eyes and let the tears come. Who will remember us? she wondered. Who will remember our lives?

She lay on her bed, reached for her red Esterbrook pen, and began to write.

Sylvan Cliffs

We moved here when I was twelve – during the war. I remember that. It didn't seem to reach us – the war. We knew no one, really, who fought. Funny, isn't it? But our family was so small – no uncles, cousins. Just us. Me, Louisa, Mamma, and Faht.

So Faht got a big contract from the army – shirts, I think. And the factory ran seven days a week. It was fun, exciting to visit. All the workers seemed happy, not sad about the war at all. At least, that's how it seemed to me. That couldn't have been the case, now that I think about it. They must have had children, husbands, relatives fighting. All women and old men now that I see it in my mind.

But they were always nice to me, and Nettie would let me bake for them – cookies, cakes, and I'd take them in, put them in the lunch room up on the second floor. They built it there because the lint wasn't so bad up there. Lint sinks. That's what they told me. and the sugar, flour wasn't so easy to get then. Everything was rationed, but somehow, we had enough. Nettie made do and Mamma was never interested in sweets anyway. So we didn't have them much to miss.

Mamma said we should move to Ellicott City. She never wanted to before, but then she learned that Sylvan Cliffs was for sale and she went to town on Faht. By that time Louisa had married Charles, and it was the three of us and we didn't need all that room, much less the grounds. But it was what she wanted.

Faht was working just about all the time, so she took over Sylvan Cliffs. That's all she thought about, talked about. When we moved, she was so focused on the house, I think she completely forgot about me. I found my new school myself.

Claire stopped, smiled at the memories, then continued to write.

Now I know that sounds crazy, like she was a bad mother, but she wasn't. I loved being around her and when we were together; we laughed and talked. She was very strong-willed, you know, like Louisa. That's why they didn't get along. When they were together – well all Faht and I wanted to do was to keep peace.

So that's how I ended up at Sylvan Cliffs. Louisa's always hated it, and she seemed to hate Mamma even more after we moved, didn't even try to hide it after that.

Claire capped her pen, sat staring at the words. Well, she thought, that's how it was, and I can't think of anything more to write. She frowned, wishing that she had ended on a more positive note. But, that's how it was, she told herself, then wondered what she would write about her next house. I'm homeless, she thought, then shook her head. Not really, not really homeless. Just without the home I love. At least I have Daniel. He'll understand

She pulled out the box filled with the ivory embossed stationery. Lily's. Claire had taken it from Lily's desk. Something to remember her by, something to use for only the most important letters, only the most important people. Daniel.

September 29, 1949

Dearest Daniel,

Well, here I am – I'm in my room. My roommate is downstairs in the lounge. She is – well, hard to know. I think we both feel – odd, perhaps? She is from Chicago and this is her first time East. I don't know why she chose to come here. I don't know why I did either – and I hope she doesn't ask. Just brochure with a picture of azaleas. They reminded me of Sylvan Cliffs. I guess this is better than the WACs – or not. I don't know why I'm here. Maybe the WACs would have been a better choice. Maybe Louisa was right.

It's so lonely here. The first time I've been away from home. All the girls are so smart, smoking, playing bridge, knitting those argyle socks. Well, at least I smoke, and I got a book on how to play bridge. So far no one has asked me, and I am both grateful and sad about that. We have compulsory chapel. I'll bet Faht will be surprised about that. He said that he wanted me to expand my thoughts about religion. Well, nobody here seems to be thinking anything about religion. But we go to chapel and then go to the smoker to drink coffee and play bridge or knit.

But mostly I miss you. And hope that you will write to me. I know how busy you are with school, so I will understand. I love you and am so glad that you love me and know that we will be together.

I plan to come home for Christmas – I don't know where I'll be staying. Don't know much about the new house. Louisa says that Faht is busy moving. She didn't say where, but I heard from Faht and he says that it is on University Parkway, right across the street from Hopkins – and you.

I think I will take Louisa's advice and not bother him. She said he has many worries and

*that my contacting him just makes it worse. She
said that she would tell him that I'm doing fine
and am very happy here.*

*I think the dorms close over the holidays. I
have met one girl from Germany who is here. Her
name is Anneliese. I've spoken to her – a lot of
the girls won't – and they make fun of her accent.
The war, you know. And her clothes, well, they
are awful. I don't think she's Jewish, so she must
have been a Nazi, or maybe not. I think that she
might be the only girl here who is lonelier than I.
I like her and I don't think that I could like a Nazi.
Well, at least she is not Japanese. I wonder if
she'll stay. Or where she will go if she leaves.*

*But meanwhile I have you. And I go to sleep
every night thinking of our kisses – and
remembering that time I let you put your hand
you-know-where. When we see each other, I will
let you do it again. Really!*

*I love you and check my mailbox for your
letter every day.*

Love, love, and kisses and more,

Claire

And then, a month later…

October 29, 1949

Dear Daniel,

*I know you are studying a lot and that is why
I haven't heard from you. It has been exactly one
month since I wrote to you. I don't want to bother
you, with your studies and all, so I haven't sent
you another letter. I do write one to you every day
though. I have saved them and will mail them all
to you in a packet – that is, if you say you want
me to.*

I think about you all the time – except for studying – and even write your name and mine in my notebook – with all sorts of curlicues and flowers around them – but I don't write "Mrs. Daniel Fourst." Well, there I just did, didn't I? I am hoping that will be the real thing. Maybe soon?

I have to tell you that I won't be home for Christmas. Louisa says it would be best if I stayed here, so as not to upset Faht. He has enough on his mind without worrying about me. I checked and I can move into the one dorm they keep open for international students while the school is closed. It will cost more, but I can pay it from the insurance money Mamma left me. Louisa is still angry about that, I think. And it probably wasn't fair. But Faht insisted that I keep it and not give it over to her, which surprised me. Maybe he sees more than he lets on.

So maybe you can come to visit over Christmas? Or maybe I could come and meet your family? I will let you touch me wherever you would like. I love you that much.

I will also try to get to know Anneliese a bit better just in case I will be in the International dorm with her for a few weeks – that is, if it doesn't work out with you to visit or me to visit your family. If I stay here I'm not sure how I'll fill my time – we are pretty isolated here – and no classes or studying. It is already lonely. I can't imagine how awful it will be if we are not together.

My first Christmas since Mamma died. I wish you were right here now to hold me, or at least hold my hand. I love you forever,

Claire

Six

Claire was one of three students who remained in South Hadley Hall for the holidays. and Anneliese stayed as well, along with a French student whose Princeton boyfriend rented a room in a local inn. They didn't see too much of her. The administration, unhappy about keeping an entire dorm open, yet bound by their commitment, did its minimum – cereal and milk for breakfast, packaged sandwiches for lunch, and a voucher for dinner at a local restaurant.

Now used to Anneliese's accent and cadence, Claire became intrigued with her newfound friend, appreciating the courage of someone who had left country and family to come, alone, to a new country.

"Oh, you know, I thought I could speak English. I was first in my class. I had no trouble filling out the forms, answering all the questions. I think they wanted students from Europe to add to their prestige. They offered me a scholarship. So, what did I have there, at home? It, well, that is for another day. This is better. Not better from before the war, but better than now. You cannot imagine."

Claire knew that she could not imagine. Being with Anneliese made her feel better about all she felt sad about. And Annaliese almost accepted that she had found a friend, a friend who wouldn't ask until Annaliese was ready to tell.

Five days before Christmas, while they filled their cereal bowls, Anneliese suggested an *Abenteuer*. "It is an adventure. I will teach you some German. Here we are, stuck in this *Dorf*. I want to see America; I want to see the city. We go to Boston, *yah*? To Boston."

Early the next morning, they sat, side-by-side, heading east on the train. They planned to stay overnight in a hotel and return the next day. Claire insisted that she pay for the hotel, since Annaliese was responsible for giving her this early Christmas present, this *Abenteuer*.

Lulled by the clack of the rails, Annaliese asked about Fritz, why Claire called him Faht. "Is that a common term of endearment? I looked for it and cannot find it in any book."

Claire laughed and shook her head. She asked her friend to tell her the German word for father, for fart.

Anneliese laughed. "You want to know those two words? Father and fart? So, this has something to do with your story?"

So Claire learned *Vater, Vati*, and *Furz* and replayed the story of her family and her Faht.

"Here's how I learned. I had just come home from school. I saw my mother, Lily, sitting at the secretary in her bedroom."

Claire knocked, gently. Lily turned and placed the green Waterman pen on the blotter. Its gold trim caught the sunlight through the window. She smiled. "Well, how was school today? Come on in; we can visit for a bit."

Claire laid her books on the coffee table and bounced onto the sofa. "Mommy, do you know what 'fart' means?" The third-grader giggled.

Lily laughed. "Where did you hear that? And you know that's not a nice word." Lily walked over to sit beside her daughter; Claire threw her leg over Lily's knee.

"I heard it at recess. Somebody farted on the playground. Really loud. That's when everybody laughed. One of the boys came over from his play yard and started singing "Fart, fart, in the yart." But whoever did it, didn't admit it. So we all looked at each other like they were the ones, not us. But it wasn't me.

"Then John Burstel started saying it too. He's the new boy who just moved here. And he said "faht." Just like that "faht." Just what we call Faht. So I knew that, first thing, I wanted to ask you if that's why we call him that. Does he fart?" Claire could not contain her giggles. Just saying the word 'fart' in front of her mother. That was something, she thought. Like a grown-up.

Lily pressed her lips together. "I would certainly say no to that one, Claire. And we must tell him your story at dinner." The two laughed. Lily put her arm around her daughter, then turned to face her.

"No, you and Louisa call him Faht because, when Louisa was a little girl, about your age, I think, they all made Father's Day cards, her class, that is. On the one she gave to your father she had written "Happy Fahter's Day." We all giggled at that and started to call him Faht. And then it stuck. So, when you came along, you called him Faht too. But no farts. Promise?"

Claire snuggled against her mother's side. "Not even if you and I whisper it? Just the two of us?"

"Not even then."

Lily shifted, sat Claire up straight. "So, you can start your homework in here. Let me get back to my paperwork. We can work together, and apart. How about that?"

Claire leaned back against the cushions. Today is a wonderful day, she thought.

"So, that's how Fritz is Faht," Claire said.

Annaliese looked over at her friend and was quiet.

"And you," Claire looked straight ahead, not meeting Annaliese's eyes. "How about you, your family? You never talk about them, your life, before you came here. What was it like?"

Annaliese continued to stare out the window, counting the evergreen trees as they came into view. Claire looked over at her friend.

Annaliese felt her gaze. "No," she said. Claire reached over to take her hand.

"I said no." Annaliese opened her book and stared down at it.

"Not to worry," Claire said, and wondered why that phrase seemed so right for the moment. She felt Annaliese relax beside her.

The young woman smiled, a genuine one. "Absolutely, *mein Freund*, not to worry." She paused. "Thank you, Claire. Really."

Once in Boston, the mood lightened. The two found a hotel near the train station and went on their way exploring. Claire could not remember laughing so much or so hard; Annaliese could not remember laughing. But that day and the day after, she did.

They trudged back to their dormitory late the next afternoon. Annaliese went directly to her room; Claire checked her mailbox. A letter from Daniel. He loves me, she thought. I know he does.

When Claire returned to their room, Annaliese was seated at her desk, writing. A letter home to Germany, Claire thought. How sad to be so far away from family at Christmas. She was quiet, did not want to disturb her, as she sat down on her bed and tore open the envelop. News from Daniel, she thought. He must love me.

Dear Claire,

It's been fun writing these letters back and forth, hasn't it? Sort of pen pals, but more.

How is school? How are you getting along? What about your roommate? Are you still liking her? I forget where she's from.

I'm sorry that you haven't been able to get home. It must be hard being so far away, what with your mother and everything. But I guess it gives you more time to study. Have you seen much of Boston? Is it cold there? Well, that's a stupid question, I guess.

Sorry that I haven't written more, but I did like getting your letters.

So, the real reason I'm writing – this is hard – since we've known each other just about a year now. Carolyn's Christmas party. And I know that we have been very good friends. And I was glad that I could be with you when your mother died.

But, you see, we are so far apart now, in distance, that is, and I am so busy studying, which I'm sure you are as well.

And, you see, I think from your letters that maybe you've got things a little bit wrong

You are a beautiful girl, and I will always remember that. But I think it is better that we keep things as friends. Do you agree? That we not be so serious about one another.

We are young and have a lot of experiences ahead of us and it would not be good to be tied down. With one another, that is.

I hope that this doesn't hurt your feelings. And that, in the future we could meet sometimes as friends. Just not now.

So, I wish you a very Merry Christmas and I wish you a successful school year.

Sincerely,

Daniel

Claire folded the pages and returned them to their envelope. She pulled back the spread and pushed the envelope under her pillow. She lay down, facing the wall, wishing that she had brought her bear with her. Then she remembered. She had given it to Charlotte to remember her by.

Seven

The waitress had taken their orders – cream cheese on date-nut bread and a scoop of raspberry sherbet.

Claire pulled the red pack of Lucky Strikes from her purse, offered one to her high school friend.

Peggy shook her head. "I just can't understand. Why would you leave? Why would you even think about leaving? You have everything there. Everything anyone could possibly want." Peggy stared at Claire, eyebrows furrowed. "All these years we've known each other, since grade school, and I knew that you'd be somebody someday, go somewhere.

"And here you are, going to such a fancy school that nobody's even heard of it, and you are actually talking to me about leaving? For what? A job at Hutzler's? Downtown as a secretary? You can't even type, for god's sake."

"I didn't say I was, Peggy. I said I was thinking about it. Just thinking, that's all. And don't, please, don't say a word to anybody, but I had to tell somebody, had to hear myself say the words.

Her friend sat, waiting. Claire remained silent. When she could stand it no longer, Peggy jumped up. "But why? Just tell me why. You're certainly smart enough." She sat, folded her hands on the table, waited for Claire to continue.

Claire looked down, picked at the ragged cuticle on her thumb, place it in her mouth, gnawed at a piece of skin. Peggy looked away. She hated when Claire did that. She didn't think Claire was even aware of it.

Claire tucked her thumb in her fist. "I'm only smart enough in some ways. Smart enough to pass, to get acceptable grades, to memorize, to learn what people, the teachers, say. But I'm not smart enough to think, to figure things out for myself. I can tell you why if someone tells me. But I can't do it on my own. I don't even know what they're talking about when they ask for my assessment. That's what they say, you know. 'And what is your

49

assessment, Miss Mueller?' I manage to stutter something out, but it makes me sick to my stomach afterwards. Really."

Claire took a breath. Peggy watched her.

"And it will only get worse. Sophomore year there are seminars, no matter which major I choose. Small groups, nowhere to hide."

"But your friends. Don't forget, I'm sure they must feel the same way."

At the word friends, Claire's eyes filled. She felt her throat tighten. "There are no friends, Peggy. Not really. There is nowhere that I fit in. And, I know, I'm from the East, I'm from a big city. That should help, and it does. I know that it's not as bad for me as for some. They don't make fun of me, at least that I know about. I don't count enough for them to make fun. I'm just invisible.

"The group there, there are two, really. They're all smart, so it's not that I'm smarter. But some, well, it's all about dates and tea dances at West Point, and getting pinned, getting engaged, getting married the week after your graduate. And I thought that's what I wanted too when I came here. I did, really. With Daniel, all of that. That's all I thought about. But when he, you know, well, I got over that. And now I do see that there's more. It's like this group knows that. They sense that I'm not like them, that I don't belong.

"But I would like to date, at least have somebody I could call a boyfriend. Everybody there is having sex. Really. All that chapel stuff, but I know. They don't even try to hide it. Proud of it, really. And the only way I think to find somebody to ask you out is to go away for the weekend with somebody who already has a boyfriend, and maybe there is somebody they have on the leash."

Peggy snorted, took a cigarette from the pack in her purse, offered one to Claire. Claire paused, lit up, inhaled. "And you see how impossible that is. How impossible everything is."

Peggy blew two consecutive smoke rings. Claire tried, failed. They both laughed.

50

"Pay attention. This is a serious matter I'm bringing to you," Claire said, still smiling.

Peggy frowned in what she hoped Claire would see as serious, nodded for her to continue.

"Then there's the other group. Intellectuals, I'd call them. I'm not smart enough for them, I can feel it. I tried once to dress like they do, you know, tights, cardigans buttoned up the back, a kerchief round my neck. But even to myself, I looked like I was dressing up for Hallowe'en.

"So, there you have it. My misery. The only person I feel really comfortable with is German. And she's more of an outcast than I am. It doesn't seem to bother her. It's something that I could never talk to her about.

"And I still have some of Mamma's money left. I should feel lucky, right? I can do whatever I want. Stay, go. But if I left, where?"

"Could you, would you want to come, back here? Come home?" Peggy asked.

Claire laughed as she blew a perfect smoke ring. "Oh, doesn't this sound gloomy. But, really, it doesn't feel like home anymore. Faht's sold Sylvan Cliffs; Louisa, well, it's been, uh, unpleasant since the insurance policy thing, before that, really. Faht told me that I needed to keep the money, all of it, not to split it with her. So I think she's glad I'm gone, surely would not want me back."

Peggy tilted her head to the left. "I'm not sure a smoke ring will help, but you know you can always stay with us, 'til you get on your feet, figure out what you want to do."

Claire shook her head. "You are such a friend to me. I would be lost without you. At least I have summer to think about it. And that job at the insurance company. Faht pulled some strings." Claire stubbed out her cigarette. "And I don't even have to type!"

The two girls left the Virginia Dare Restaurant and headed in separate directions on Howard Street. Peggy turned to wave goodbye "See you next week." "I want to be sure to hear your plans. Just don't be dumb."

Claire shook her head, wondering if whatever she chose would turn out to be dumb.

Eight

Eight quarters. Claire put them into four piles and spoke into the receiver. Sunday rates, at least four minutes. She could say it in that time. She had rehearsed it, keeping her voice calm, no tears.

Fritz picked up on the fourth ring. He stood by the demilune beside the front door. He was startled to hear Claire's voice, asked first if she were all right.

"I'm fine, Faht, fine." She cleared her throat, faced the wall of the first-floor corridor. "It's just this, ah, that I wanted to talk to you about. Rather than a letter. Or wait for a visit. It's..."

Fritz stared at the oil painting on the opposite wall of the foyer, one of the few he had brought from Ellicott City. "Something's wrong. Tell me. We can work it out, figure it out. Tell me. Don't worry, just tell me."

"Faht," Claire swallowed. "I want to leave school. I hate it here. I hate it. I have no friends, well, only one, and she's German, and no one talks to her either. And now she's leaving, moving to New York. So there will be no one, not one person for me." Claire stopped, waited for two juniors to walk to the parlor. They nodded as they passed her. Claire struggled to get her breath.

Fritz was silent. "Are you sure this is what you want to do? You'll finish your second year, at least. Don't waste that. Then do you want to come home? What are you thinking about doing?" he paused.

"Clairedelune, I know what it feels like to be miserable at school." He thought back to his boarding school days. "But this is the first time you've mentioned being unhappy. Did something happen?" he considered his next words, aware of her silence. "Is it a boy? Did something happen?"

Claire laughed. "Oh, Faht, I wish it were a boy. I could get over that, I think." She realized that she was feeling calmer, calm, actually. She placed her right arm above her head, leaned into the wall. Fritz heard her exhale.

53

"No, it's not that. It's – well, I've written it down. I'll send it to you in a letter. Then we can talk. Really, I feel better now. Just hearing your voice. I miss you, Faht. Since Mamma died, I've hardly seen you. It's always Louisa, Louisa doing this, doing that, telling me what to do, telling you what to do. And you doing it. It's like you have forgotten that I'm your daughter too." Claire waited for tears. They didn't come. She had said aloud, and to her father, the thoughts that had been with her for two years.

Fritz closed his eyes. "Oh, Claire, that's just not true. You know it isn't. How could I ever not think of you? You are my baby, Claire. Don't think that I don't love you.

"Do you want me to come there? I could see you this weekend, fly up. We could talk."

"Oh, Faht, I didn't mean to hurt you. I guess I needed to get it out, to say it. Please don't say anything to Louisa. I guess I'm feeling lonely. I'll write to you. Don't worry, I won't go anywhere, do anything drastic. I actually like most of the classes. It's a lot of work. I'm just not as smart as I thought I was. They tell me everyone thinks that, so there I guess I fit in."

"I worry about you, Claire."

"Don't. No need for that. Really." Claire pulled herself erect, felt imagined that string from her head through her pelvis, like Miss Lynn, her ballet teacher at Peabody, had drilled into her. "Faht. I'm feeling much better. Just talking to you has helped. A lot. Really."

With assurances of love on both sides, Claire ended the conversation and returned to her room, pulled her letter to Fritz from her notebook and tore it into pieces. She placed the pieces in her jewelry box.

Fritz walked to the kitchen and took the casserole from the oven. Louisa had left it for him.

A week later Claire pulled her shoulders back, inhaled, and strode toward Annaliese's room. As usual, the door was closed. Biting her lip, she tapped her fingernails on the door. A cloud of smoke enveloped the pair as Annaliese opened it.

"Do you have a few minutes? Are you alone?"

Annaliese nodded and closed the door behind Claire. Easing into her desk chair, she turned to face her friend.

"What is it? The little chicken needing advice? A shoulder?"

Claire cleared her throat, a laugh caught up in it. "No. Nothing like that. More a decision. Already made. And I want your opinion. Honestly."

Annaliese chuckled and blew a perfect smoke ring. "I only give honest opinions."

Unsmiling, Claire clasped her hands in front of her, unconsciously following her years of education with the nuns. "I'm leaving school. I'll finish out the year, but then I'm done. I've put in two years, all I can stand. There's nothing more for me here, and I'm ready for a new start, fresh. Like you. Your bravery has rubbed off on me. Maybe." Claire stopped, hoping for a smile from Annaliese.

None came. Annaliese stubbed out her cigarette. "Whatever you think is best for you."

Clare smarted at the flat delivery of her friend's response. She felt a room heavy with silence.

Annaliese raised her right eyebrow. "Really, chicken, I think it's fine. If you've thought it through. Are you sure you want to go home? What would you do?"

Claire started. "Home? Oh, no. I'm going to New York. Like you."

Annaliese remained expressionless. She studied her fingernails, noticed where the polish had chipped on her little finger. "Of course, it is a free country, no? America? So you can move wherever you'd like. And New York. City of opportunity. *Yah*. That might be good for you, I think." She paused. "But, you know, I cannot be your, what? overseer? babysitter? It is fine for you, but do not expect me to make sure that happiness finds you. I am not so good as a guide in that regard."

Claire felt her eyes fill. She had hoped, expected, her news to be greeted with smiles, laughs, Annaliese's bottle of schnapps to appear for a celebration. She walked to the window, noticed the trees coming into leaf.

"Well, no, I don't expect that. But we can, we will, still be friends. Our living in the same city won't change that." Claire paused. "Will it?"

Annaliese watched her friend, her only friend, if truth be told. And Annaliese always told the truth, to herself at least. This privileged, naïve child, she thought, and found it impossible to hate her.

"Of course we will be friends," she said. "Here, in New York as well. So, maybe we both find lodging at the Barbizon. Not together, of course. But there. They tell me it is a safe place for women on their own." Annaliese stopped. "And you think you are ready to be a woman?"

Claire smirked. "Where is your schnapps? I'm ready for a bottle of my own."

Annaliese laughed aloud, then reached into the bottom right-hand drawer of her desk. Holding the bottle high, she toasted, "*Prost*."

The next evening Claire called Fritz. He hung up with a smile, then sent her a twenty-dollar bill with a note:

> *Your mother would be so proud and excited for you. As am I. I'm as close as a phone call and a short train ride.*
>
> *Love to my Clairedelune,*
>
> *Faht*

Nine

By June, the two women were in New York. Annaliese found work before she left Mt. Holyoke, in the office of an international food brokerage. Claire, keeping an eye on her dwindling savings account, found a part-time job at Macy's. Her salary did not cover her lodging, and she searched the newspapers' want-ads every morning.

They lived on separate floors at the Barbizon Hotel for Women. Both understood and accepted, Annaliese more easily than Claire, that their lives were heading in separate directions. Annaliese had a suitor. Claire thought that he might be German. Or Dutch. Or from someplace over there. Annaliese didn't say. Claire knew enough not to ask, and wondered how and where she'd found him.

After six weeks, Annaliese moved out. "Too much," she said when she told Claire. "Too much knowing my business, too much telling everybody how to act, what to value.

"A finishing school. I'm already finished, more finished than I want to be. But you, chicken, this is good for you. A haven. You need that."

Annaliese looked at her friend. "We have been good for one another, I think. Yes. It has been good. But that part is over, behind us. Now we are different. We will keep in touch, no? But not so much." She leaned, kissed Claire on her left cheek, near her mouth.

"*Auf Wiedersehen*. You know what that means. Until we meet again."

Claire sobbed, unable to respond.

By Thanksgiving, Claire's hours at Macy's had increased. She was next in line for a full-time position. Things, she thought, are looking up.

But the following Wednesday, Claire stood in the elegant lobby of the Barbizon. She gently pushed down the buttons on the phone to end the call. She held the receiver, still damp from her tight nervous group, to her forehead.

No answer. A gift from what, who, she thought. God? The universe? I had to call, talk to someone. And who else to call except Louisa? I can't burden Faht with my problems, this disgrace.

She choked trying to hold back tears, and looked around the hallway, breathing a grateful sigh that she was alone. I need to hear a voice, family, she whispered to herself. Annaliese. Annaliese would knock some gumption into me.

She hadn't seen her friend in months, had seen her only twice since she moved to Greenwich Village. She's with her beau, Claire suspected. And no telephone number that she knew of. Annaliese had written her those times they had seen each other. Claire accepted that Annaliese wanted, needed, to keep her distance, her privacy. She knew that was how it had to be. Annaliese, her fear of intimacy, Claire thought, as she remembered reading that term in a past issue of *Ladies Home Journal*. But today, she missed her friend, that stoicism, that sternness that presented her with a strength that Claire hadn't realized that she possessed. More tears came.

"I am so lonely." Claire was startled to hear her own words, and quickly looked around, grateful that no one was there to overhear. She covered her mouth with her hand so that no further words, thoughts, could escape.

Counting the minutes until she could be alone in her room, she walked toward the elevator. Let me think, work it out. I'll imagine Annaliese is here with me, imagine Annaliese telling me to figure it out, figure it out for myself.

But she was not to be alone. Claire saw that someone was there, waiting for the elevator to arrive. Shirl. If it has to be anybody, Claire breathed, good that it is Shirl. They had been quiet friends, Shirl offering a smile on the evening that Claire moved in, Claire clapping with genuine delight when Shirl announced a job in the chorus of *Paint Your Wagon*.

Claire recognized a shyness in Shirl, though no one would suspect. Such poise, confidence, Claire thought, and wished, hoped, that she presented that same demeanor. She worked hard to copy and emulate it. And this day, this hour, Claire felt a connection.

"You look beat," Shirl said. Claire started to speak, then heard the rasp of metal rate of the elevator door as it opened.

The two smiled at the operator as they stepped in. No need to tell her their floors. Francine knew the girls and their locations. Sitting back on the velvet-covered stool, she gave the two a once-over. "Looks like I'm not the only one who's had a hard day."

Claire felt herself smile. This must be what they call gallows humor, she thought. Placing her handkerchief in her cuff, she looked at Francine. "I surely hope that yours was not as bad as mine."

The car stopped at the 19th floor. "Most like as not, Miss Mueller. But a good meal will make it better. And a good sleep."

"And maybe a large shot of gin," Shirl interjected.

Francine laughed, a soft laugh that belied her demeanor. "Now I ain't saying nothin' against the rules. That's for you important girls to decide."

Claire stopped before she left the elevator, turned. "Do you have a minute? Can you stop in before dinner?" Francine knew the question was not directed to her.

Shirl nodded and followed Claire to her room. "I meant what I said. Do you have any gin? You look like you could use some." She moved the pile of Claire's books from the wing chair to the floor, then flounced into the seat. "This has got to be about a lover. Tell all." She folded her hands in anticipation.

"Oh, god, if only it were about a lover." Claire was surprised that she could laugh, that she no longer felt like crying. I am, after all, she thought, a sophisticated New Yorker now. If you live in New York City, you don't cry. She sat down on the bed, nudged off her black suede pumps, unfastened her back garters.

59

"Well," she started. Unexpected tears appeared. Claire wiped them away with the back of her hands. "Oh, Shirl, I've lost my job. they fired me, just like that. No warning. They called me into the office, the little one at the back of the floor. Told me to get my things. They would mail my last check, pay me though the end of the week. It felt like I had five minutes to leave, no time to say goodbye to anybody, not that there was anyone I wanted to tell.

"What will people say? They'll think I'm some kind of a criminal or something." Claire pulled her handkerchief from her sleeve, wiped her eyes.

Shirl jumped up. "What? Why? Who did that? Do you want me to go down there? I will. I'll cause a stink. All they can do is tell me to leave."

Claire laughed as she blew her nose, noting the blotches of black mascara on her handkerchief. "Shirley, you can make the worst seem funny."

Shirl sat on the bed to Claire's right. "I know. I don't mean to make light of it. This is terrible. Especially for you. You take everything to heart." She placed her finger on Claire's knee. "But after you get over the shock, who knows, this may not be so bad. It's not as if you wanted to end your days selling men's underwear at Macy's."

Claire leaned against the headboard and sighed. "I know. You're right. It's just that it was, is, such a shock. To be fired on the spot. I've only read about things like that. I never thought it would happen to me."

"What did you do, anyway? Smuggle out a sleeveless tee shirt? Try on a pair of briefs, or boxers, over your clothes?"

Claire giggled. "If only. That, at least, would have some drama." She laughed some more. "No. What I did was file receipts, those reports that I fill out in triplicate. Well, I must have put the carbon paper in backwards, so, the second and third copies, the ones that go to the buyer and billing, I think. They were blank. There must have been at least a hundred of them. I've been doing it that way since I started.

"I don't know what I was thinking, or not thinking. And so, my career in retail appears to have come to an end."

Shirl bounced on the bed, clapped her hands. "Oh, Claire, that is the best. Much better than wearing men's underwear outside your clothes. It'll take Macy's months to find all those invoices.

"You deserve a double gin for that. Wait here and I'll bring some down. We can have a pre-prandial drink to celebrate. What a story you've given me. And you. You'll see. This time next week you'll be laughing about it too. I promise."

Claire looked over. "You are absolutely the best."

Shirl pulled the door closed as she left; Claire unhooked the rest of her garters, pulled off her stockings, and lay back on the narrow bed. Leave it to Shirl to make an adventure of all this. I wish I had her confidence, Claire thought, but then I'm the one who's lost her job, not her.

No job. No boyfriend. Only three dates this whole time, and then no second dates. Claire closed her eyes, held her breasts in her hands. No boyfriend. No future. No money.

"What am I going to do for money?" she said aloud. Standing, she counted her steps as she walked toward the window, looked out at a brick wall. Maybe, she thought, I've had enough of New York.

Ten

Claire had set the small table in the dining room the night before; she brought in the wrapped gift and placed it under the tree that took up the southeast corner of the living room. Not exactly Sylvan Cliffs, she thought, but it will have to do. Something to cheer Faht, a Christmas breakfast, like the old days. Except it would never be like the old days, that she knew.

But the first year was the hardest, she told herself. That was behind them now, this the third Christmas without Lily. She was surprised how little the holiday mattered to her. Just a day to get through, a dinner to endure. She shook her head and walked to the console that held the record player and moved the needle to replay the Mario Lanza LP, a gift from her to Fritz that first Christmas-after. Funny, she thought, how now we measure Christmases from Lily's death. I guess that's how it is, and she wondered how, or if, Louisa felt sadness, loss, ever.

She sniffed the scent of Fritz's aftershave, Old Spice, an odor she'd later recognize from the favorites of her lovers. His bedroom door opened, and Fritz emerged, always dressed as if he were expecting, or attending, a party of swells.

"I thought I heard you rustling around," he said, as he came over to kiss his daughter. "Merry Christmas. We can make this a good one, yes? Each year a little bit easier."

"Merry Christmas, Faht." When, she wondered, could it just be Christmas and not an anniversary, not counting the years since?

"So, a light breakfast before we head to Louisa's? What do you think? I want to swing by and say hello to August. We won't stay, but it means a lot to him."

Fritz paused. "I want to present you with your gift here, just the two of us. It's a big deal."

He sat forward in the burgundy damask chair, one he had brought with him. "Such a year this has been for you. Such adventures. And now, starting on yet another. What would Lily have thought?" He walked to his room and returned carrying a bulky carton topped with a red bow.

Claire clapped her hands. "Faht," she laughed. "This better not be a set of pots and pans."

Fritz set the box on the coffee table. "Better than pots and pans. I think you'll get more use out of this." He watched as Claire plopped down on the floor and pulled off the ribbon. Still such a little girl, he thought. And a woman. He could see nothing of Lily in her. Her own person, he thought. Good for her. Since Lily's death, she has really been on her own. Here for a bit now and then. But New England, college, New York. All on her own. And now back here, back home. And he wondered what would be next for her.

Claire brought in a kitchen knife to open the carton. Pulling the flaps back, she reached in. Fritz steadied the carton as she removed its contents.

"Oh, Faht. This is the best. A record player. My own record player." She turned it around and opened the lid.

Fritz beamed at his daughter. "Look at the front. There's a radio in it too. Everything you need."

Claire leaned over and kissed her father's cheek. "Really, this is absolutely the best gift. Something to take with me..." She stopped.

"I know. You don't have to tiptoe around it. Something to take with you when you get your own place." Fritz scratched the back of his head. "But I hope it's not too far away, so that you can come home, come by, ah, well, so that you can visit as often as you please."

"Oh, don't worry about that, Faht. I'll want to be close to Hopkins for my night courses, and you're right across the street. And I'll stay here for a bit. I need to get on my feet, get so that I don't feel butterflies every morning at work. Then will be time for a place. For now, you can count on seeing me for dinner every night.

"And thank you for this, Faht. You couldn't have picked a better gift." She rose to her knees, leaned over to the tree. "Now, let me give you your gift. It can't compare to my," she looked over at the phonograph, "my Zenith, but you know it carries just as much love."

Wrapping paper removed, Fritz held the light blue box. "Tiffany's. Oh, Claire, this really is too extravagant."

"Open it. I used my last paycheck, some of it anyway, from Macy's. It made me happy to be able to do this. So you can think of me every time you light up."

Fritz opened the box and removed the silver lighter. He saw his initials: FAM. "Even engraved." He kissed Claire's hand. "You put a lot of thought into this, Clairedelune. And yes, I will think of you every time I use it."

Don't talk about Mamma, Claire thought. Don't. Let us be here, now, without memories. She jumped up, went to the closet to get an apron, one of Lily's that Fritz had brought with him.

"So, how about coffee, juice, and some of the stollen you brought home from Lexington Market? We can take whatever is left to Uncle August's. And then have an appetite by the time we get to Louisa's."

Fritz nodded as he went to his desk to fill the lighter with fluid. He pulled a pack of Chesterfields from his shirt pocket and lit up. Every time. I'll remember Claire, he thought.

"Well, shall we toast the prodigal daughter?" Louisa said as the group sat down to dinner.

Claire felt her throat clench and looked down at her plate. An awkward silence filled the room.

"What's prodigal?" Charlotte asked, as she held her champagne flute filled with ginger ale. When no one answered, she looked around and repeated her question.

"Hardly prodigal," Charles responded. He lifted his glass. "Let's say we should toast a welcome home to our *bon vivant* sister, aunt, sister-in-law, and daughter. A true woman of the world."

With a relieved breath, Fritz clicked his glass with his granddaughter. "Oh, yes. *Prost.*" The women at the table remained silent, not making eye contact with one another.

Charles, determined to save the occasion, soldiered on. "So, Claire, you have a job lined up, I hear. But I don't know any details. Tell us about it."

Louisa considered leaving the table but decided to stay. It's Christmas she thought. I can get through this. She bit down, hard, on her thumb. "Oh, yes. A big shot with the Health Department."

Claire interrupted her. "Oh, hardly that. Really just a clerk. But it's a start. You know that the Baltimore Health Department was the first public health department in the entire country. The very first. So, it's very historic. And it was really Faht who got me the job."

Fritz interrupted. "Now, I didn't get you the job, Claire." He turned to Charles. "I met the director when they were looking at some possible expansion sites. I merely gave him a call and told him about Claire. She got the job on her own. I merely, what, greased the skids there."

"Yes, but if you hadn't put in a good word, they wouldn't have even considered her."

Charles looked over at his wife. "Louisa, not today. Let's be happy for Claire now that she's back home with us."

"And you'll be going to school too, won't you? So we'll both be going to school, just not together." Charlotte waived her goblet in Claire's direction.

The group, except for her mother, laughed. "I can see that sweet Charlotte is going to be very comfortable at cocktail parties," Fritz said.

"Call me Charlotte Russe, Faht. Like you call Clairedelune."

Claire beamed at her niece. "Where in the world did you hear about Charlotte Russe?"

The child sipped her drink. "My teacher. She said that it was a dessert. You can be a song and I can be a dessert. That way we can be together, related."

Ignoring her daughter, Louisa continued. "Well, maybe you'll be able to meet someone when you're at night school. All those men with the GI Bill going to school. And what about Daniel. Is he still there? Or have you gotten over him dumping you like that?"

Fritz threw down his napkin. "Louisa, please."

Claire laughed. "Oh, no, that's fine. I am certainly over him. Puppy love, right? Everybody has that once. Once."

She swallowed. "Then they grow up and get on with life. And that's what I'm doing. Though I wouldn't mind meeting a fellow at McCoy College, that's what they call the night school at Hopkins. I'm counting on being surrounded by men, day and night. After all, I'm almost twenty-one."

The men broke into relieved laughter. Claire joined in, not knowing where the chutzpah she exhibited came from. I like it, she thought.

"I'm almost twenty-one," Charlotte sang, while all but one present breathed a grateful sigh for her trusting innocence.

As the two drove home, Fritz looked over at his daughter. "You handled yourself like a pro today, Claire. I'm proud of you."

Claire laughed. "I'm proud of myself too. I'm not sure where it came from, but I would surely like to it return. And often."

When they got back to University Parkway, Claire carried her phonograph to her room. I'll need some records, she thought, and started to make a list.

Eleven

August died in January.

Fritz called Claire at work to tell her. "He had a good life. Not an easy one, but a good one. And he was like a ..." Fritz's voice broke.

"I know, Faht. I know." And for yet another time, Claire saw that her father was human.

Fritz was the executor of August's will, and was surprised that to learn that his godfather had less wealth than he, than most, thought. August had stipulated that twenty-five percent of his assets go to various German charities in the city; Fritz received the balance.

Fritz walked to the window of his office, looked down on the cars blocking Fayette Street, thinking of the many times that August had been there for him. A confidant, a financier, an advisor. It was he who steered Fritz to this job in commercial properties. Where would I be without him, Fritz wondered, and realized that he would rather have August in his life than his money.

Fritz lit a cigarette, using Claire's lighter. August, I hope that I've made you proud.

Twelve

She was in her own place, her home, hers. A studio apartment, 3rd floor, but it had a bay window and looked out onto Calvert Street. An eight-block walk from the Hopkins campus, she had time for a quick supper at home or a hot meal at the Blue Jay Restaurant before her evening classes. The registrar gave her credit for all her Mt. Holyoke courses, and seemed impressed with her grades. He didn't ask why she left, but she had been ready with an almost-truthful response.

The campus was as crowded in the evenings as in the daytime hours. Seven years after war's end, veterans, GI Bill in hand, struggled to make their way in the business world by day and academic realm at night. To Claire, these men seemed ancient and world-weary, less-than-engaged in what literature had to offer. A bit contemptuous of the professors, until they learned where they had been in the war. It's like they want to keep it alive, but not talk about it, Claire thought. To her, it remained a world away.

Two courses each semester, four nights a week, one course in the summer, the registrar told her that she could finish in four years, maybe three if she could keep up the pace. It seemed forever to Claire, but she didn't want to let Fritz down, and she enjoyed the books, the comments from her friends who couldn't understand why she was wasting her time like that. It set her apart, and that made her proud. To be different. But it also kept her apart, isolated.

At her job, there was never enough to do, and it took more energy to pretend to be busy than if there had been actual work. The other girls didn't seem to mind, in fact, Claire thought that they enjoyed complaining about how burdened with filing they were.

She knew she didn't fit in. Just one more place, she thought. Her coworkers mistook her shyness for snobbery and made fun of her clothes, which they viewed as too expensive, too stylish for girls working in an office awash in carbon paper smudges and splotches of mimeograph ink, while also noting that she really only had three outfits. Miss Peck and Peck, they called her.

She was lonely. Lonely around people, she thought, the worst kind of lonely. She chatted with her Hopkins classmates during their mid-session breaks, though none suggested anything beyond that. She saw friends from high school occasionally, but they were married now, except the two who had entered the convent. And Claire could be only so interested in recipes and curtains and husbands; even Peggy was lost to her now. She feigned interest in their children, was godmother twice over, though her belief in God was minimal. Her friends sensed her indifference, and the invitations to Sunday dinners, to meet eligible men, dwindled and then disappeared.

I wanted to be just like them, Claire remembered. Daniel, fantasies of a one-bedroom apartment in Bolton Hill, complete with forest-green velvet Victorian sofa, she wearing a white apron edged in Battenberg lace as he came up the stairs each evening after work.

She smiled. I am on the campus, just like Daniel had been, though she knew that McCoy College didn't carry the panache of The Johns Hopkins University. She wondered how her diploma would read, and made a note in her spiral notebook to find out, putting a paper clip at the top as a reminder.

Well, she said to herself, I have an apartment, not in Bolton Hill, and not quite an apartment, but, still, here I am, on my own.

She looked over her room – a single bed, the one she had since childhood was tucked against the far wall. Faht had it delivered from his apartment, along with a chest of drawers when she moved in. He had found a drop-leaf table in, as he called it, an antique shop on Frederick Road. Claire knew it was a junk shop but didn't correct him. The size was perfect to hold her hot plate, and came in handy as a desk and a table for her few meals there.

They found two chairs on another South Baltimore expedition, a wingback with a firm cushion, the other an ample, soft, saggy chair, too big for her small space, but roomy enough for Claire to curl up and read.

"I think next week I can find you a television set. I worry that you're lonely here," he had told her.

"Faht, really, no. I need to study and I think it would be a distraction right now. And I do have my record player, and some records. But later, for Christmas or my birthday, I wouldn't say no. You don't want Louisa to be upset that you're giving me all these things. I can manage on my own, you know." Claire smiled and touched the top of her nose.

Fritz was surprised by this gesture. My Clairedelune is growing up, he thought, an appealing, self-assured young woman. He shook his head. "Pay Louisa no mind. You know how she is. And she means nothing by it."

Claire did not respond. They both knew this not to be the case.

Thirteen

Claire worked to steady her breath as she walked down the long narrow corridor to the Director's office, told herself that it was not the same as that last encounter at Macy's, that she would not be fired. Then she thought, well, possibly I will be. There was not enough work for all of the clerks. Maybe he knows that. She was the last hired. First fired, she thought and tried once again to get her emotions under control. She would be Annaliese. Annaliese would never let such things get under her skin. Never. I will be as strong as Annaliese, Claire said to herself.

She entered the secretary's outer office. "Dr. Watson asked to see me?" Without glancing up from her typing, Jane Dudley nodded and indicated that Claire should have a seat.

"Be sure to make friends with the secretary." Claire recalled Fritz's words to her. "You always want the boss's secretary on your side. Without it you're on an uphill climb."

Claire smoothed her skirt and looked up expectantly. "I am so nervous. Do you know what he wants? Why he called for me?" She tittered. "Of course you do. You know everything that goes on here." Oh, why did I say that, Claire thought. Just keep quiet. This is not the way to make a friend. "Uh, I don't know why I said that," Claire continued, unable to keep silent. "I'm just so nervous."

Jane stopped typing, looked up. She shook her head. This one doesn't fit in, she thought. This one would have been gone by year's end. "You might be surprised. It may be a good surprise. You never know."

"Oh, thank you for that." Claire folded her hands in her lap, willed herself not to giggle. This is not Sister Clotilde. You are not being called into the principal's office. You are an adult. Stop acting like an idiot. And, for the first time, she thoughts about her boss's name. Watson, Dr. Watson. My dear Watson. She blinked hard to keep herself from laughing out loud.

So occupied was she with herself that the tall, thin man standing in the doorway of his office had to repeat himself.

"Ah, Miss Mueller, is it? Please come in. I hope you haven't been waiting long."

Claire followed him into his office, stepping around the manila folders that appeared to Claire to be strewn on the floor around his desk.

"No mind to them," he said, and indicated the chair at the side of his desk. Claire sat, knees clamped together, hands folded in her lap. Try to look comfortable, lean back in the chair, she told herself, then found her instructions to herself to be impossible.

Watson began. "You've been here, what, four months now?"

"Three and a half, sir," Claire responded, then swallowed. She continued with her voice in a lower register. "It has been a great opportunity for me. I have learned a lot."

Watson, looking at the file he held in his right hand, ignored her. "And you have several years of college, I see by your application."

"Yes. Two years. And I'm enrolled at Hopkins, at McCoy College, and am taking two courses each semester. At least that is my plan." As Claire spoke, she realized that she had interrupted Watson. "Excuse me, sir. I didn't mean to interrupt."

The stern gentleman continued. "I'm happy to see that you're continuing your education. It fits with what I am about to propose."

He watched for Claire's response as he continued.

"There's a program in the works, a joint effort between us and the Hopkins School of Hygiene and Public Health. The research will be done by senior staff, of course, but we need someone who can be the liaison, to be responsible for making sure that information flows quickly and uninterruptedly between the two departments."

Claire waited for him to continue, hoped that he couldn't hear, or see, her heart beating.

"So. I have talked to your supervisor. She has nothing but good things to say about you, that you are quiet, a bit solitary, but a levelheaded worker." He looked up from the folder.

"Is this something that you think would appeal to you? Working with the two entities? Hopkins and us?"

"Oh, I love hygiene," Claire responded, and immediately regretted her words. "I mean the School of Hygiene, Public Health, Hopkins, I mean. Sir." Half-choking, she stifled a chortle. "Oh, yes. I would be very interested. And I am a very hard worker. Conscientious. Yes." She forced herself to stop talking.

Martin Watson smiled. "Well, I think yes as well. The program is just getting underway. It would be good for you to meet the trial leaders. They can choose a start date for you, but I think it best if you be part of the meetings from the beginning." He picked up his phone.

"Jane, would you set up a time for Hancock and Rothberg and Miss Mueller to get together. In my office. I'll stay for the first ten minutes. They can move to Hancock's office after that."

He stood. "I'm glad that we had the chance to meet." He stood. "And salary. Let us discuss that. I'm authorizing a three percent increase starting…" He stopped, waved his left hand in the air. "Just talk to Jane. She takes care of those details. And give my best to your father."

Claire hesitated, considered his last words. "Yes. And thank you so much for this opportunity, Dr. Watson. I will do my best."

"I'm sure you will. And, if you would, close the door as you leave."

Claire willed herself to walk sedately from the office. When she saw Jane, she said, "You knew about this, didn't you? Thank you so much for your kind words. This is just the best day. One of the best ever."

"I'll let you know when the meetings are set," Jane responded crisply, reaching for the phone to dial the Hopkins number. As she waited for Rothberg's office to answer, she looked over at Claire.

She'll have to toughen up to get through this one, she thought, and wondered how long that young innocence could last.

Fourteen

Claire heard the telephone as she entered the foyer. Putting on an extra burst of speed, she pounded up the fourteen steps while she pulled the keys from her coat pocket. Throwing the door open, she threw her purse to the floor and lunged for the phone.

Before she could articulate a breathless hello, she heard Louisa's voice. "Well, it's about time you got a telephone. It's been almost impossible to contact you."

Claire plopped down on the wing chair, pulled the phone onto her lap. "I just wanted to make sure I was able to afford it. I wanted to be here a few months to see just how much it cost, to live here, on my own." Claire swore to herself as soon as the words left her lips. No need to apologize, Claire, no need to apologize or explain. You are an adult, she thought.

She heard another voice. "Old habits die hard." Great, she thought, now I'm hearing voices in my head that aren't even my own.

She heard a snort. "You, worried about money? Why don't you use your inheritance, the money your mother gave you?"

Claire sat holding the receiver to her ear. She chose not to respond.

"Well, that is neither here nor there, is it?" Louisa continued. "I called because I need you to babysit Friday night. You can take the bus right from work, spend the night, or Charles can drive you home if it's important to you to return to your rented room." Louisa emphasized her last two words, and Claire received the message.

"Oh, Louisa, I'm so sorry. But I can't do it Friday." She stopped, then added, in a voice softer, higher-pitched than she liked. "Would Saturday work? I could do Saturday."

She heard Louisa breathing. "I was counting on you, Claire. Charlotte was looking forward to it. What do you propose I tell her? That you're too busy to see her?"

Claire felt her heart pound. Stay silent, she told herself. Do not respond while you are feeling this way.

"Well?" Louisa said.

"Louisa, I'm so sorry about this, really I am. And I hate to disappoint Charlotte. Maybe she could come, I could come to get her on Saturday and she could spend the night here. It could be an adventure for..."

Louisa interrupted. "And just what do you recommend I do about Friday? Tell me that."

Claire took a deep breath. "I suggest you look for another baby sitter."

She heard Louisa slam the receiver. Claire put the receiver to her mouth while she laughed and cried at the same time. She decided that she needed an evening off from her classes. She went to her bed and lay down with her arm over her eyes. She'd call Saturday morning.

Ten minutes later, she went to the phone, dialed the number. "Louisa, I can babysit Friday. It's okay."

"Well, plan on spending the night. I don't want to ask Charles to take you all the way to your room. He's worked hard all week. You can take the bus on Saturday morning."

Louisa paused. Claire heard a gentle voice. "Thank you, Claire. I know Charlotte will be delighted to see you."

Claire returned the receiver to its cradle without replying. Then the tears came. "Such a hold she has over me." Claire said these words aloud, then closed her eyes.

Part Two

Fifteen

Claire focused on her job, on her classes, her quest to lose her virginity never quite neglected. No deflowering took place, and the blind dates her friends arranged made her glad she was single.

Maybe this is the way it will be for me, she thought, and worked to make peace with that. I've finished my degree at Hopkins. Maybe I'll just be one of those career women. Maybe somebody will write an article about me someday.

Still, her eyes remained open for eligible men. Apparently, they did not keep their eyes open for her.

She steered clear of Louisa, and Louisa was content to allow that, as long as she had no need for someone to stay with Charlotte in the evenings.

But then a phone call to Claire at work, an invitation extended.

Whatever she wanted, Claire knew that it wasn't good, this Saturday lunch invitation.

Claire arrived at Hutzler's Colonial Room as Louisa was giving her name to the hostess. The sisters had a short, uncomfortable wait before they were seated toward the back of the restaurant, a corner table.

"Choose what you want quickly. I don't want to waste time looking at a menu," Louisa said.

Claire laid the menu card on the table and started to speak.

"Wait until the waitress takes our order. Then we can talk." Louisa frowned as she spoke.

Their orders taken, Claire squirmed in her chair, trying to inch over the garter that pinched the back of her thigh. She sipped at her water, feeling her stomach rumble. It was not from hunger, that she knew.

"Did you know about this? Did you know and not tell me? Did Faht tell you to keep this from me?" Louisa tapped the middle finger of her left hand on the table with each question.

Claire worked to keep her face expressionless, all the while feeling heat rise to her cheeks. "What are you talking about? What about Faht? He's not sick, is he?" Claire regretted her questions as soon as they left her lips. Louisa could always spot a lie, Claire thought.

"You'd better be telling me the truth." Louisa picked the polish on her nails, all the while staring directly at Claire, watching, working to decipher her expression. Claire was always a lousy liar, she thought. She placed her hands in her lap.

"It is Faht. He's not sick. It's worse."

Louisa knew that silence made Claire uncomfortable, that it would quickly wear her down, put her where she wanted her. She counted to fifty before she began, watched as Claire's face became flushed.

"There is a woman," Louisa laid her palms flat on the table, "trying to get him in her clutches."

Claire clapped her hand over her mouth as she heard a nervous giggle escape. Seeing Louisa's fury at her response, she felt her heart race, then exhaled with a barely-stifled sigh of relief. She said nothing, knowing that whatever response she gave wouldn't placate Louisa. Unless she agreed with her, there would be war. She closed her eyes, willing herself to say something that would smooth the waters. No words came to her. Whatever she said would be wrong, trouble.

Their soups arrived, tomato for Claire, mushroom bisque for Louisa; Claire picked up her spoon, concentrated on the food before her.

Louisa's expression darkened. "Well, what do you have to say for yourself? Do you plan to sit there like a ninny? Always trying to please everyone, never taking a stand." Louisa's fist hit the table as she spoke, enough that the silverware jumped. "I need you to stand up against her, stand with me, get her out of Faht's life."

Claire looked at her sister. "I don't know how to do that, Louisa. Maybe she makes him happy. It's not like he's being disloyal to Mamma. She's been gone, well, years now."

"Do you really think I'm worried about your mother, her memory? This woman is a gold-digger. She after his money, that's all."

"I don't think you're right. She seems very nice. Faht seems happy. And I don't think that he has that much money, really. I don't think he'll marry her. I have a feeling he won't marry again. He loved Mamma."

Louisa's eyes narrowed. "She seems nice?" Her voice rose. "She seems nice?" The three women at the table closest to them turned. "You know. You knew." Water spilled from the goblets as she pushed herself back from the table.

"I always knew you were a sneak. What? Did you put him up to this? Did you arrange this? Miss Goody-Goody." Louisa rose, her soup untouched. "You can just go to hell," she said. "And you can pay the check. Use your inheritance."

Louisa headed toward the front of the restaurant, then turned back. "And you haven't heard the last from me" she said, loud enough that all eyes turned. When she reached the hostess desk, she screamed, "You've seen the last of Charlotte. I'll be sure to tell her what a traitor her aunt is."

Claire sat at the table, eyes down. The waitress came with a cup of tea. "Thought you might need this, sweetie."

Claire smiled her thanks.

Sixteen

Fritz stood at the living room's oblong window, the pinks and oranges and yellows in the early evening sky complementing the plaid pattern of the draperies. He heard the apartment door slam. He knew he should go after her; Louisa would expect it, sure that he would comfort, soothe her by saying that she was his favorite, would always be his favorite, that it would never change, explain that no one could ever replace Lily. No, he thought, Lily, saying Lily's name, that would have made it worse.

He remained at the window, wondering if, how, it could be worse. I should never have started this, he thought, this charade, should never have allowed it to continue. *Who's the fairest of them all? Tell me, Daddy. You are. Louisa is the fairest of them all.*

He heard her delighted giggles, saw her twirl in the pink net tutu that Lily had scoured Baltimore to find, a Light Street costume shop finally providing it, for a price. Louisa's fifth birthday. He thought that she had loved Lily once, when she was such a little girl, but even then, it was in her own way. He wondered when it all had changed, when Louisa had changed, when she had become filled with such anger. So different from Claire, not like any other child he knew.

Oh, Lily, help me, help me handle this. He thought back through the years, the bouts of Louisa's temper, when she wouldn't let Lily get near her, screaming at her mother to get away. All that rage. And Lily, was she hurt by it? A few times she tried, Fritz remembered, a tentative step, then backing away, from Louisa's indifference, disregard. An armistice, Lily called it, the right side of her mouth always twitching when she said the word.

And the trio managing, most times, acclimating itself to Louisa's ignoring Lily. Why did we let that go on, focusing on other things, a relief when Louisa retreated to her room, her radio, her books.

A truce of sorts. Fritz remembered how he would call Louisa to his study, review her homework, attempt to pry some information about her day. Lily would bring in a snack, milk, a cake, and reach out to touch Louisa's hair, looking for, though not expecting, a connection. Always an edge of sadness to Lily, he thought. Louisa's edge was anger, a fury simmering beneath the surface, unleashed by what? Neither Fritz nor Lily knew.

Fritz leaned against the back of his chair. I recognized it then, he admitted to himself, and I chose to look away, to retreat to the quiet of books once the women in my life were asleep. Peace, he thought, how much I longed for peace. He rubbed his forehead. And how I ignored the price that others paid.

He stood, walked to the entry door, opened it. The hallway was empty. Fritz realized then that he thought Louisa would have stayed, that he would find her sitting in the hallway, like a child. He lifted the door mat. No note. He exhaled, more relieved than disappointed.

As he turned, he thought of Claire. Dear, sweet Clairedelune. With her arrival, Louisa had drawn new battle lines. Fritz knew this would be so. He remembered those discussions with Lily. What it would mean to have this baby, bring it into this world, this family. But Lily convinced him. *This is a chance to have a child who loves me, whom I can love.* And Louisa, she said, maybe it would change Louisa if she had a brother, a sister, someone to take care of. Fritz smiled. Lily could convince him of anything.

Claire, who loved everyone, who wanted to please, who ached to be loved, arrived. And Louisa turned darker, with everyone, except Fritz. He and Lily saw it; Fritz tried to talk to Lily about it, but Lily only talked of Claire. *She's no trouble and she lights up every time I enter the room. It's like I've made my penance and this is my reward. She adores Nettie, and Nettie can do her work with no problem. She told me she loves tending to Claire. It's all worked out, Fritz. I can't believe how lucky we are, how we made the right decision, to have her.*

On those rare occasions when Lily acknowledged Louisa's behavior toward her younger sister, she was thoughtful. *Most likely it's a combination of jealousy and adolescence. It's understandable, Fritz. And really, it's not that much different, she's not that much different, is she? As long as we keep Claire out of her way. Louisa has her friends, her schoolwork, her boyfriends. So many boyfriends. That should make her happy. And she's agreed to let me take her shopping for some prom dresses. So maybe she's growing out of it. Now that she's older, maybe, finally, she'll be better.*

Fritz closed his eyes, saw Lily standing before him. "Come," he said, reaching to pull her onto his lap. "Louisa will get over it, won't she, Lily? If I just give it a day or two, she'll be back to normal."

Fritz heard himself speak and shook his head to remove the memory. Then he went to the phone to dial Louisa's number. To make sure she arrived home safely.

As she pulled into the driveway, Louisa saw Charles standing in the doorway. She felt her heart seize. Charlotte. Something has happened to Charlotte. She turned off the ignition, crying and calling as she ran to him.

"No, no, Charlotte's fine, just coloring in front of the TV. But Fritz called. He was worried, said you had left upset. What happened? He wants to know if he should come by."

Louisa shook her head as she entered the house. "Where's my Charlotte?" she called out.

Charlotte jumped up and ran to her mother, surprised and delighted to hear her words.

"There's my Charlotte!" she said. "You are fine, no worries for you." Louisa leaned to remove her daughter's arms that encircled her knees. "Go back to your work now," she said. "Show me the pages when you are finished."

Charlotte, keeping her eyes on her mother, sidled back to the table where her crayons lay. Louisa threw her purse on the table by the door, shifted out of her coat. Charles took it from her and placed it over the chair, waiting for his wife to continue.

"Let's move to the kitchen. We can talk there."

And so he heard how Louisa had gone to Fritz to tell him how upset Claire was about his woman; how Louisa tried to help him understand that he shouldn't be involved with someone who was just simply after his money; how Louisa was there to make sure that he had a good life, to look after him.

"And do you know what he told me? Do you know what he said? After all I've done for him?" Louisa banged her fist on the table. "He said that he would talk to Claire, but that he didn't think it was Claire who was upset, that he didn't need anyone to take care of him. Asked me why I would ever think that.

"After all I've done for him, all I've given up for him." Her voice broke. "So ungrateful. Told me that I needed to face facts, that someone had to tell the me truth, that I needed to concentrate on my own family, put them first."

Louisa paused to catch her breath, reached up to smooth her forehead. "Oh, I know Claire's involved in this, encouraging, fostering his relationship with this woman. I know she's the one behind it."

Charles stood by the back door, looked out at the black night before he half-turned. "Then it really isn't Claire who's upset by this, is it?"

Louisa strode across the kitchen to confront her husband. "Whose side are you on? Why can't you support me? Why can't you take my side, be with me? Why are you always against me?"

Charles shook his head, kept his left hand on the doorknob. "Let us not do this, not now, not with Charlotte in the next room."

"Oh, it's always Charlotte you're worried about, never me, never me first." Louisa ran to the living room, grabbed her purse and rushed out the door. Charles heard the car start, then went to his daughter.

Charlotte was watching the door. "Where did Mama go? She left her coat. I have my pictures to show her."

83

"Just an errand. She'll be right back. Meanwhile, how about if we go upstairs and I read you a story before I tuck you in for the night."

An hour later, Charles sat on the far end of the sofa, as she knew he would, *The Caine Mutiny* open but unread on his lap. He looked up as he heard the key in the lock.

Louisa stood in the doorway, as he knew she would, and waited for him to speak. Both knew that she would break the silence.

This dance we do, he thought, and closed the book.

"Charles," Louisa said as she moved to the sofa, sat close, put her head on his shoulder. He moved his arm to put it around her. "I know, sweetheart. I know."

Louisa looked down at her hands. "I'll let Faht know I'm okay." She stood up and walked toward the telephone. "I'll call Claire tomorrow."

Seventeen

Two weeks later, Hancock called Claire into his office. She intended to ask Jane for the story before she went in, but Hancock's secretary kept her eyes on her typewriter as Claire entered the area. "Do you know what he wants?" Claire asked. Jane continued to type, not looking up.

Shaken, Claire rapped gently on the half-opened door.

Hancock stood as she entered and indicated that she should sit in the chair directly across from his desk. Claire's heart beat faster as she sat. He reached into the middle drawer of his desk and withdrew a manila folder. He cleared his throat before he spoke. Clearing it again, he began.

"Claire, as you know, uh…" He cleared his throat a third time before he continued. "As you know, your work has been, uh, exemplary." Claire fought a wave of nausea. She stared at the form he held in his left hand. Fired, she thought. I'm going to be fired.

"Yes, exemplary. And you have done well here, with this project." He opened the folder. "So, it has been decided that you will continue, as you have done before, but not here, not working with, rather, for, me. So." He used his middle finger to adjust his glasses. "So, it has been decided that you will continue with this project not here, but at the Hopkins campus, the hospital campus, exclusively. And that you will become an employee of the School of Public Health.

"So, you see, this works out well for you. Their pay scale is a bit different, so it will mean a slight raise, but still a raise. That is good, yes?" He looked for the first time at Claire.

She swallowed and nodded.

"Now, the Hopkins position calls for a Master's degree in Public Health. So, this poses a bit of a problem." Hancock stopped. Claire waited, not moving, not speaking, not breathing until she had to gasp for air. She closed her eyes, hoping that Hancock did not notice.

"Ah, so, we are in the process of working that out. But you will have to pursue that degree if you are to stay in the position. Does that fit with your plans?" Hancock closed the folder, straightened the gold lighter on his desk.

Claire exhaled so loudly that she startled herself. Once again, she been holding her breath. "Oh, Dr. Hancock, absolutely. This is such a surprise, such an honor. I was, well, I was certainly not expecting this. I just don't know what to say. Thank you, thank you so much."

He took his time lighting a cigarette, held it between two fingers of his right hand. "Yes. It is best if you start right away. We have arranged for you to start on Monday."

Claire gasped, closed her eyes and willed herself to be calm, professional, waiting for Hancock to continue. He stood and extended his hand across the desk. "You have a career ahead of you, Claire. I wish you the best."

He shook her hand and returned to his desk, her signal that the meeting was over. Claire knew not to gush. She rose from her seat, pulled her shoulders back, stood tall, thinking that her posture made her look, if not feel, like an adult, a professional, which now, it seemed, she was.

"Thank you again, Dr. Hancock. I will never forget all that you have taught me." Hancock nodded, looked down, and picked up his phone. Claire knew the drill. Meeting adjourned.

When she saw Jane, Claire smiled. "Did you know about this? That I'm going to the School of Public Health?"

Jane looked over her typewriter at Claire and nodded to her to close the door. "Sit down for a minute." She waited while Claire pulled a chair close to the desk. Jane turned to face her. "I really should not be telling you this. It could get me fired, but I'm going to trust you. Because you need to hear this; you need to know this.

"You really dodged a bullet. I don't know if you sleep with a four-leaf clover or what, but you came up smelling like a rose with this one." She watched Claire's face, saw only confusion.

"Here's the story. Somebody sent a letter to Hancock's wife – and sent the same letter to the Personnel Office here. Handwritten. I saw it. It said that you two were having an affair. Personnel called him on Monday. And somehow between now and then he managed to work this deal for you. He must have called in more than a few favors.

"I don't know who, if anybody, there knows about this, or why the transfer went through so fast, but you need to know. You need to watch yourself and watch your back. I'm only telling you this because I don't believe that anything went on between the two of you. I have a pretty good sniffer where that's concerned and I think Hancock's a straight arrow. And I think you're too, ah, I was going to say stupid, but now I'm thinking a better word is naïve. But somebody is out to get you. I don't think this was aimed at him, but you never know. So look at this as my going-away gift to you. You're a good kid and I think you could go places. A woman going places. I would like to see that."

Claire felt her face flush, felt her eyes fill with tears, willed herself to be calm. "Oh, Jane, there was never anything between Dr. Hancock and me. He's almost old enough to be my father."

Jane willed herself not to smile, but allowed a bit of a smirk to take over her face. "Well, not in the planet you live on now, at least. But watch yourself, if you can figure out how to do that. I'd be all business and leave some of that pensive sweetness you radiate at the entrance on Wolfe Street." She rose from her desk and walked toward Claire. "You know, I'm not a hugger, but you, well, you I hug. And I wish you luck." She reached for a folder on the corner of her desk. "Here's the information you need – where to go, and all that stuff. You'll get your last paycheck from here in a couple of weeks. And enjoy that raise."

Claire softened into Jane's embrace. "You know you're a peach, right?"

"Yeah, yeah. Just get on with your life. And tone down all that sweetness."

Claire saluted and laughed as she left the office. She felt tears come, so she didn't turn around to wave goodbye.

As she packed her few belongings, she thought back to a conversation with her sister. Louisa had called her the day after *the incident*, as Claire now remembered it, at Hutzler's. Louisa had seemed unusually interested in her job, asking who her boss was, what title he held, if he were married, had children. At the time, Claire thought it was Louisa trying to make amends, and welcomed what seemed to her to be sincere interest. She closed her eyes. She wouldn't do that to me. That would be too much. Even for Louisa.

But she couldn't forget that phone call. Who else knew? Who else cared enough to want to hurt me? The others at work? They seemed to have moved on, forgotten me. And no one looked askance when I told them that about the transfer. Claire was sure she would have noticed any sidelong glances.

Louisa. Who else could it have been?

Claire spent Saturday morning crying about it. By mid-afternoon she realized how Louisa's plan, if it had been Louisa's plan, had backfired. She, Claire Mueller, had received a promotion. And a raise. And would be working at The Johns Hopkins School of Public Health and Hygiene. She could call herself a researcher, maybe even get a graduate degree.

Giggling to herself, Claire went to the cabinet where she kept her supply of butterscotch Life Savers, removed the bottle of whiskey she kept for hot toddies, and poured two-fingers worth into one of her best glasses, one of a set that Fritz had given her, from Sylvan Cliffs. Flopping down in her armchair, she raised the glass to the window facing Calvert Street. "Screw you, sister." And she downed the glass,

Laughing through her choking, she went to her closet to choose her wardrobe for the next week.

Eighteen

"You know you don't need to have these cleaned every time. Just have them pressed. They'll come out the same and it'll save you wear and tear, plus a bunch of money.

Claire looked up, grinned at the clerk standing behind the counter. "You are right! I never thought of that." She tilted her head to the right. "Thank you so much for telling me."

The woman shrugged, and tagged the pile Claire had brought, three skirts, a jacket and a sweater. "Just lookin' out or those who need lookin' out for. But this sweater needs to be cleaned. A wine stain?"

Claire nodded and rolled her eyes. "A glass too many and a joggled arm, I'm afraid. But thanks again for the tip. I'll be sure to tell everyone about you." Claire hitched her purse on her shoulder and spun around to face the door. She waved as she headed to the corner to wait for the bus that would take her to work.

A few weeks later, at a must-attend cocktail party given by one of the School's major donors, Claire, crystal highball glass in hand, and aware that her gait was unsteady, carefully placed one foot in front of the other as she walked into the kitchen, hoping that a glass of cold water would restore some needed balance. As she stood at the sink, a voice behind her said, "You'll be bringing that dress back for a cleaning, not just a pressing, if you don't watch out."

Claire felt herself snap to attention. She turned. The woman from the dry cleaners, wearing a black-sequined shift, a bit too snug around the middle.

"Caught red-handed," she laughed, pouring the drink into the sink and turning on the cold-water tap. As she filled the glass, she said, "What a treat. What are you doing here? My name's Claire, by the way."

"I know your name. From the cleaning tags." Handing Claire a deviled egg, she added, "Here, eat this. It'll help soak up the alcohol. And I'm Naomi."

Taking the egg with her left hand, Claire extended her right. "Good to know your name. And it seems that you're always around to help me out." Wiping her mouth on a napkin that she had picked up from the kitchen table, Claire spoke. "I'm here from the School, for the School, really, filling in for a 'person-who-matters.' He had some family emergency, so they must have had to scroll way down the line before they contacted me to fill in. I just need to make sure that I'm seen, then I'm heading off."

Claire reached for another deviled egg, topped it with a cucumber sandwich, and set both on her napkin. "Sorry, I should have eaten before I came." She chewed, swallowed, then asked, "So, how do you know the host?"

"Oh, good god, no. I'm not a guest. I'm here helping out Janice with the food. But I thought I'd dress up just for the fun of it. This is from my store. I'll put it back on the rack tonight." Naomi handed Claire another napkin. "Don't spill. Unless you have so much money that you want to give it to the cleaners. And grease doesn't come out all the time."

"You have a dress shop? Where? I'll be sure to stop by."

Naomi laughed. "Not a dress shop. I sell all sorts of things. Used, very-well and sometimes not-so-gently used things. You could call it a junk store. Plus, I sell a bit of hard-to-find items to a select clientele."

Naomi raised an eyebrow. Claire knew that she was supposed to understand this gesture. She didn't, but nodded and put on what she considered her "wise" expression.

Claire paused. "So you are at the cleaners and have a shop too? You do all that?"

Naomi shook her head. "Oh, girl, you don't know the half of it. A little bit here, a little bit there. And a cobbled-together living."

She watched Claire's face. "Oh, don't look sad." Naomi shrugged her shoulders. "I make out just fine. After all, here I am, talking to you, right?"

The two women stood silent, Claire looking into her water glass, Naomi watching her. "I get to take home all the leftover food. Janice gets the booze. An even trade, I think. Want to share supper?"

Claire nodded her head with a sharp shake and wrote down Naomi's address. "Oh, I can walk there from my house. What time? And I'll bring the rest of the whiskey I have at home. It'll give us about one weak drink each." She giggled. "And I'll wear something I can wash myself."

Claire smiled to herself as she waited for the bus to take her home, realizing that she was lonely for a friend, a friend who was different, a friend who wasn't married, or engaged, or someone like me, she thought, or not like me at all. What a character she is. And I like her.

A few hours later, holding a slip of paper with Naomi's address, Claire turned right at the corner of St. Paul and 25th Streets. Mid-block, she saw it. *Odd Types*. I love it, she thought, and admitted to herself that Naomi was right. I would have called it a junk shop. As she neared the building, she studied the doorframe for a bell. She must live above her store, Claire thought.

She was still looking for a bell when she heard a voice as the door swung open wide. "There you are. I was keeping an eye out for you."

Claire proffered the pint bottle of rye. "I couldn't find the bell. I'm so glad you saw me."

"Well, there is no bell. Just me." Naomi ushered Claire in. "Keep walking; I live in the back."

Claire swallowed a hiccup of fear. Here goes, she thought. You told yourself you wanted new experiences. She expected to find Naomi's answer to a gypsy caravan, and was surprised to find an ordered, almost austere, living space. Crystal glasses waited for their drinks; canapes rested on a small silver tray; petit-fours were arranged on a two-tier Dresden plate.

Naomi responded to Claire's compliments by saying, "You never know what you're going to get. I have someone who's coming in this week, interested in buying the lot. So I'll be sure to wash them in hot, hot water when you leave."

Claire slouched down into the tufted rose-colored wing chair and laughed. She poured four fingers of whiskey for each of them, emptying the bottle. Claire realized that she was talking nonstop, while Naomi, her receptive listener, cheered, and snorted, and listened. Mainly the two laughed. They talked about family, about life, about men, and Claire found herself sharing the most gruesome of her blind date experiences.

"I haven't had that many really," she said, emptying her glass and running her index finger around its rim. "But they've all been bad." She told Naomi about the scientist who was on his way to great fame because he somehow managed to turn chicken droppings into chicken feed.

Naomi whooped. "Shit into gold. I hope you invested in his company!"

"You know, I had decided that I needed to lose my virginity by the end of that year. And there he was. But I just couldn't shake the vision of his hands full of ...well, you know. And he really wasn't bad looking. But, I just couldn't, not with a chicken man." Claire collapsed further down on the sofa cushions not caring that her mascara was sure to be halfway down her cheeks.

"Then there was the guy who picked me up in his gold Cadillac. Can you imagine? Me, dating someone who drives a gold Cadillac." She shook her head. "Though Mamma would have loved it. She loved all the glitz she could muster. Lily. Her name was Lily."

Naomi watched, said nothing.

"So, like it or not, I'm still a virgin. But you can't fault me for trying." Claire caught a glimpse of herself in a gold-plated mirror leaning against a wall. She was laughing, then she smiled so widely that her face ached. She couldn't remember the last time she had felt as free. Free to laugh, to drink, to tell almost all. She said nothing about Louisa.

"Now tell me your story, Naomi. It can't be as pitiful as mine."

"Oh, dearie, that is for another day. Tonight is all yours."

The women toasted one another with their empty glasses. Claire splurged on a cab ride home.

Nineteen

On this bright Saturday morning, the sun sparkled through the east side of the bay window Claire had washed the night before. Whoever washes windows at night, Claire had asked herself when the idea came to her. Well, why not, she decided, and grabbed a few pages of that day's *Morning Sun*, wet them, and climbed on a chair to get the job started.

She admired her handiwork from her bed. Just the right thing to do, she thought as she plugged in the kettle on for her instant coffee. Follow your instincts, Claire. Be spontaneous. Learn from Naomi, even if it's just washing your windows at night.

She moved to the window and studied Calvert Street, the houses, the cars as they passed. Grateful for an early start, she pulled on an old pair of green plaid slacks from her high school days and a favorite yellow sweater that had a hole under one arm, invisible if she kept her elbow down. She sat at the table to plan her morning. I'll have breakfast at the Blue Jay, then to Eddie's, then pick up a Schmierkase from the bakery, the last a treat for an afternoon of study. This time more demanding than her undergraduate work, she now worked alternate Saturdays and one night a week to make up for the day-classes she was required to take. No one at work mentioned this arrangement, but all knew it was not the norm, that she was somehow special. Claire remembered Jane's warning, and was diligent with her work and circumspect about her life.

She pulled the rolling basket from behind the door and started off, first checking the mirror by the door to make sure that no traces of lipstick remained on her teeth, and headed north, giving a nod, not for the first time, for the line of stores a few blocks from her room. My apartment. She corrected herself, even in her thoughts.

As she turned onto St. Paul Street, she stopped to look at the white building mid-block. It had been one of her favorites since Fritz had considered moving there when he left Sylvan Cliffs. *Saint Paul Court.* She loved the sound of it; she loved the courtyard; she loved the fountain in the middle of the entranceway, one that almost always worked. She crossed the street to have a better look, hoping to catch a glimpse of one or two of the rooms, should a tenant want to take advantage of the sun and pull their curtains open.

Here she was disappointed, realizing that she stood at too acute an angle to see anything. She walked further north on St. Paul Street, and as she approached the courtyard entrance, a flutter of white caught her eye. Claire stared at the sign swinging on its wooden post: *Apartment To Let. Inquire Within.*

Two children, a girl and a boy, came toward her, one on roller skates, the girl pushing a red scooter. Claire stepped out of their way and looked at her watch. Too early, she thought. I'll think about it over breakfast and decide. And I would just be asking about it. I'd never be able to afford it.

She signed the lease the following Tuesday morning. They had it ready for her at eight a.m. so that she would miss only her first hour of work. Claire took that as an omen, a propitious one.

She had told no one, had not even discussed it with Fritz. She knew what he would say. There was not one instance she could think of that he had not encouraged her to "step out and up." That was the phrase he used, when she left for Mount Holyoke, when she moved to Manhattan, when she told him of her promotion. And so, she thought, that is what I have done, stepped out and up. She would call him that afternoon, ask if they could meet for dinner.

And, she realized, soon she'd be able to invite him to dinner. She'd have a kitchen, a real kitchen. Claire had included that in her calculations. The rent was double what she paid for her room, for she now admitted to herself that hers was a room, not an apartment. Here, at Saint Paul Court (she still giggled to herself when she said that phrase in her mind), she'd have a kitchen, her own kitchen, and a bathroom all to herself. She could hang her stockings, her brassieres, her girdles, anywhere she chose. She'd buy a drying rack.

Then there was the dining room, a huge dining room. And draperies. The ones from the former tenants would work fine. In her seat on the bus, she pulled out a pen and started yet another list. No major purchases for a while. Get used to the expenses first. A kitchen. Pots, pans, dishes. And rugs. She would need rugs. The manager insisted. Faht would definitely be a help with that. She would take her bed and chairs. But she would choose the rest of her own furniture, when it came time and she knew she could afford it. That she would choose on her own. Potthast's. One piece at a time, 90-days-like-cash. That was a start. Bit by bit, that's how I'll do it. Nothing too fast, nothing extravagant. Still, she thought as the bus turned onto Broadway, I live at Saint Paul Court.

Arriving at her office, she dropped her purse into the bottom drawer of her metal desk. This is it, she thought. A job, graduate school, an apartment. On my own. Really on my own. She sat at her desk, retrieved the pack of Lucky Strikes from the middle drawer, and lit up. Leaning back in her chair, she blew a perfect smoke ring.

Annaliese, how long has it been? she thought, surprised to feel tears spill over. She took a handkerchief from her purse. Look at me now, dear Annaliese. Oh, my friend, I wish you well.

Twenty

Claire turned the knobs on the radiators in the living room and opened the door to the bedroom to dispel the morning chill. While she appreciated her views of the city, the south-east exposure meant her apartment never really warmed up during the day. That, she thought, should be a good thing when summer comes.

Her days, her evenings, her weekends, remained full. Work, study, more work, more study. Claire had called Louisa twice since her move. The first time, there was no answer; the second time she had spoken to Charles, who said that he would let Louisa know that she called. Claire felt more relief than regret, and even more relief that Louisa hadn't called back.

When she told Fritz about her promotion, her arrangement with her graduate courses, he was full of congratulations. Claire assumed that he had told Louisa, although her name never came up when she and Fritz were together. At first, they had met for dinner every week. Then the intervals increased; Claire had little time for herself now. But they talked a few times each week, if only to check in. Nothing was said of Fritz's friend, as Claire thought of her, and Claire saw now how many things she and Fritz avoided talking about. She had not told him the reason behind her transfer and promotion, of her conversation with Jane, her suspicions that it had been Louisa who had written those letters. She had said nothing of the last time she had seen Louisa, the lunch at Hutzler's all those months ago. So separate, so apart, she thought. And Fritz had not confided in her, about Louisa, about his private life.

And now the holidays were upon them. The best and the worst times for families, Claire thought. Since Lily's death, Christmas and Thanksgiving had been spent at Louisa's, Charlotte giving the family something happy to focus their attentions on. But so far, Fritz had said nothing about the approaching holiday, and Claire hadn't asked. Such a pattern with us, avoiding anything unpleasant, she thought. Concentrate on the job and your courses, she told herself. If you dread a holiday, it's your choice on what you want to do with it.

Finally, in mid-November, over a quick dinner at Jimmy Wu's, Claire broached the subject with Fritz. "We should probably talk about Thanksgiving, Faht. Has Louisa said anything? She and I haven't talked in a while."

Fritz reached into his pocket for a cigarette, took his time lighting it. Never a good sign, thought Claire. He looked at his daughter. "Has something gone on between the two of you? Have you seen her since she was so upset about, well, you know?"

Claire placed her knife and fork on her plate. "I haven't. I called twice. I don't know if she's tried to reach me, you know I'm gone a lot. She doesn't have my new number at work. And, well, there, it's, ah, it's complicated. It always has been with her, don't you think?"

Faht shook his head. "I just can't get in between you two, Claire. You know how it is." He stubbed out his barely-smoked cigarette. "Maybe it would be best if you came over for breakfast, for a fancy breakfast on Thanksgiving, at the apartment, you and I. I'll cook. Then you'd have the rest of the day to see your friends, or to study. That might be the best thing, don't you think?"

Claire nodded and looked down at her plate. The lump in her throat precluded her having any dessert.

Thanksgiving hadn't been as bad as she had expected. Fritz had come by the week before, bearing a portable television set and Claire accepted it without even a "oh, you shouldn't have." His breakfast feast was sumptuous, replete with food, laughs and love. There was something freeing, Claire decided, about knowing where you stand.

When she talked to Fritz the next week, she didn't ask about Christmas plans. Christmas hadn't been the same since Lily had died, not even Charlotte could make up for that. "So, should we do a repeat of Thanksgiving for Christmas? Only this time, let me do breakfast, just the two of us."

Claire sensed Fritz's relief over the phoneline, though she did cry when they hung up.

And the day came. Claire had shopped over the past weeks, stocking up on fancy German imported foods, stollen, hazelnut yule logs, lebkuchen; Fritz brought an apple tart. They exchanged gifts, a shirt for Fritz, and a Turkish carpet for her foyer for Claire. They made the most of their time together. They talked easily about past Christmases with Lily at Sylvan Cliffs, laughed about the time Fritz tried to roast a goose. Louisa and her family were never mentioned.

After they had said their goodbyes, Claire straightened up and washed the dishes. I guess this means that I'm now officially an adult, she thought. I'm having my own Christmas.

But she cried when she thought about Louisa, and wondered what Charlotte was doing. A death without a death, she thought, then busied herself preparing for dinner. Naomi was coming. Claire smiled, anticipating the tales her friend would bring.

Later that Christmas night, the two sat in the chairs by the window, relics from Claire's Calvert Street days, their bohemian sags a bit out of character with her new, not-quite-paid-for Danish Modern sofa.

"I didn't think you could pull it off, but you outdid yourself tonight." Naomi raised her glass and rattled the ice cubes.

"All helped by your generous gift of bourbon, I must add." Claire laughed and rested her head on the chair's arm. "What a year it's been. And I am ever grateful that you've been such a big part of it. I know I couldn't have – well, I could have gotten through it, but without nearly as much courage if not for you. So thank you for that. To say nothing of the money I've saved on dry cleaning!"

The two sat, quiet, each with her own thoughts. Finally, Claire broke the silence. "So, tell me about you. Really. How you became who you are. How you got so strong."

Claire threw back her head and laughed until she chocked.

"Oh, Naomi, where were you when I was growing up? I'd be a completely different person had I known you then."

Naomi had just finished the story of her name. She leaned back in the chair, she had always loved yellow, and laughed again.

"Shirley Naomi. Can you imagine a mother giving a child such a name? She must have known even then that she'd pass on no good traits to me, no favors, starting with my name.

"Shirley. When I got to school, there were six girls in my class named Shirley. The teachers, all through eighth grade – none of them really could ever figure out who was who.

"So that did it. I left school and left Shirley. Not so many Naomis. The bible, mind you. My mother wouldn't have known that. She must have heard it somewhere and it stuck. Or rather she stuck me with it when somebody must have reminded her that the child needed a middle name.

"None of the ones that came after that got one. Just me. A lasting gift from the poor sucker. Had so many children 'til she ran out of names. I guess that's what stopped her. And him. He was gone so much he just must have come in the door for a fuck. Then gone again. John Barleycorn his best friend. None of us every really knew him.

"Hagerstown during the Depression. The only good things about it were the streetcars and the Maryland Theater. Movies for twenty cents, and the trolley man would let me ride for free. I guess they knew I wasn't going anywhere. I'd just get on and ride, anything to get away." Naomi shook her head.

"Oh, yes, the library was the other good thing about that place. That's where I learned about people who were famous, who lived real lives. Yes, I should say the library, and the people who worked there. They were the best about living there.

101

"I worked in a barber shop, sweeping, until I had saved ten dollars, all in one-dollar bills. I packed a pillow case with my things. Can you imagine it? A pillow case. Went to the bus station, and by afternoon I was in Baltimore. Never told a soul, and my mother didn't come after me. She probably was glad, relieved that I went, except for the pillow case. She would have wanted that back.

"So, here I am, just sitting with you, Miss Up-and-Comer. Now no one would have ever thought that I'd have a friend like you." Naomi rattled the ice in her glass and finished the last half-inch of bourbon.

Claire shook her head and smiled. "You are my hero. Grit and guts." She raised her glass. "Cheers!"

Naomi looked at her watch. "Six minutes to get my bus. I checked. They're running a limited schedule today. Can't afford to miss it." She took her coat from the rack by the door.

"Next week, my place. We can ring in the New Year."

Naomi hopped from one foot to the other as she shivered in the wind that tore down Charles Street; Claire watched from her bedroom window as she rounded the corner for the bus stop, then returned to the dining room to clear the table.

Another Christmas, she thought, and wondered what Fritz was doing.

Part Three

Twenty-one

Claire faced Louisa across the table. Their conversation, as it inevitably did, turned to Lily. Regardless of how it started, it always came to Lily and Louisa's diatribes. Claire pushed her plate toward the center of the table, laid her forearms on the table, and, waiting for Louisa to take a breath, looked at her sister.

"Louisa, I've asked this over and over. Why do you hate Mamma so much? I understand that she wasn't perfect, wasn't the mother you wanted, or deserved, but she's dead. She's been out of your life for years, years now. Why do you torture yourself?"

Louisa put down her fork. "You are pathetic. As always, you take up for her, spend your time being the perfect daughter. Well, you don't fool me. I know who you are, what you are."

Claire felt her chest tighten. She promised herself that she would not give in, not this time. She inhaled, closed her eyes, thought of Naomi, how she would respond.

"What have I ever done to you to make you hate me like this? Why do you try so hard to hurt me? When will it be enough?"

"Oh, there you go. The victim. Cinderella and the ugly stepsister. The good one and the bad one. You're always sure to be the good one, you sneak, you phony.

"You're a liar and a thief, and you know it."

Claire felt the tears come. "What have I ever stolen from you? What? Why do you say that?"

Louisa pushed her hand in front of Claire's face. "My ruby ring." She waved her fingers. "You stole my ruby ring. You went into my room and stole my ring, and they did nothing about it, said that you were just a baby, that you didn't know any better. But I knew, knew that even at four years old you were a thief. All those tears, and I was the one who got punished when they found out that I disciplined you. A just punishment when she would, she chose to, do nothing.

"You say that I beat you. Prove it. Go ahead. Prove it. You have nothing. The word of a maid, nothing. So, you see, it didn't happen, you brat of a troublemaker.

"I was always the one who was punished. Never you. And she was delighted to do it. Got pleasure from it. I saw it. I know. She always wanted to be sure that Faht saw me in a bad light. She was always telling him that I did bad things. She was a liar too, just like you. You and she are alike, just alike. You are her."

Louisa screamed these last words, turned in her chair as she used the back of her hand to wipe her face. Claire sat, silent, torn between seeing her sister suffer and wanting to go to her, comfort her.

Louisa turned back to the table. "And then she left you an inheritance. That was the final slap in the face. And you took it, kept it. Faht thought that I should have it. He told me that, that he asked you to give it to me, and that you refused. You are just like her.

"He said that too. He said that you are no different from her. Trash, that's what you are, nothing but trash."

Claire sat without moving, raised her right eyebrow. "So it's all about money? It's about money?" Claire, surprised by an icy façade that she almost felt, knew that her unruffled bearing was inflaming her sister, and enjoyed the scene and her role in it.

"She owes me," Louisa screamed. "She owes me. That money is mine."

Claire answered before she had a chance to think. "Money? You think money will change things? Is that what you want, the money she left me? And Faht told me to keep the money. I was going to give it to you, or at least half of it. It was Faht who said no, that it should be mine, that you were well-established, those were his words, well-established. You need to give some thought to just who is the liar in this family. If he said it. If you did not make that up. If that was just a scene that you concocted in your head."

Louisa, suddenly calm, faced her sister.

"Thank you for a lovely lunch, Claire. You have certainly improved as a cook." She paused. "And since you offered to give me the amount that your mother left to you, I must say that I will graciously accept. I agree with you that it is the right, the honest, thing to do. I'm glad that we can agree on that."

Claire picked up the plates and walked into the kitchen. Louisa walked toward the door, turned to speak.

"I'll expect my inheritance in cash. I don't trust any of your checks. Before the end of next week. If I don't have it, you will hear from my lawyers." Louisa paused. "My legal team."

Claire heard the front door close. She leaned across the sink and pressed her head against the window. It cooled her warm forehead. She stared out at the alley and noticed a rat as it scampered into one of the wooden garages.

Later that evening, Claire stared out at the lights of the automobiles on St. Paul Street. She felt that pull, so familiar, to be at home, to stay home, alone, safe, and realized how often it came to her, at times like a surge, an Ocean City wave, when she had ventured just a bit too far off shore. A wave that threatened, yet felt encompassing, secure. No one can get to me here, no one can find me. I am safe here, she thought.

She took in a deep breath. "Not tonight, Clairedelune." These words she said aloud, then shook her shoulders. She thought of Naomi, and remembered Annaliese, those strong, free-spirited women who had these qualities she longer for. Ah, the fox and the hedgehog, she thought, and stamped out her cigarette before she walked into the bedroom. I hope I'm not destined to be the hedgehog, she thought, afraid that she already knew the answer.

Twenty-two

Three days later, Claire threw back her head and laughed until she choked. They sat in the second-floor apartment above Naomi's new business.

"Call it a junk shop. Forget all those fancy names. These are antiques, all right, but only because they're old. They were cheap then, and they're even cheaper now."

Claire smiled as she kicked off her shoes and loosened her back garters. She had come from Naomi's directly from work.

"Next time bring some comfortable clothes; the neighbors will wonder why I'm entertaining such posh guests."

"Oh, Naomi, where were you when I was growing up? I'd be a completely different person had I known you then."

It had been a month since Naomi had settled with the previous owner, the mortgage secured with a bit of a word from Claire to an acquaintance who had an acquaintance with a savings and loan officer. The first-floor shop remained as it was, chock-a-block with bureaus whose drawers stuck, iron bedsteads, wooden headboards that had seen more than their share of owners. But the apartment, at the top of a steep, narrow stairway, was a life removed from the life of shoppers needing a crib, a bed, patrons who didn't mind that someone, or many someones, had used them before. Except for the plumbing, a few rodents, and the war on roaches, that is. For when Claire's friend sat in her living room, each piece acquired one-by-one over the years, a buttery yellow chintz-covered sofa and one soft yellow chair, a braided rug she found in an alley, one wall of books, special to her and read, or would be read, someday, she seemed to be just who she wanted to be, and it was this, and her freedom, and her salty, uncensored language that Claire loved. Claire knew she would always get a straight answer from Naomi, and she confided in her as she had never done before.

Claire leaned back in her chair. "So tell me, what do you think?"

"Well, she's just a jerk. And crazy. And jealous. Don't you see that? How can you not see that, as smart as you are?"

Naomi stubbed out her cigarette, reached over and took one from Claire's pack. She leaned back and tapped Claire's foot with her own. "Oh, I know you're hurting. I don't mean to make light of that. But step back and see it how I see it. Now, I can't believe I'm saying this, but this is not normal. I may not know what normal is, God knows, but I know what it's not – and this is it.

"She's just plain nuts, Claire, or as you might say, 'troubled.' She's taking it out on you. Who knows why?"

Claire pulled her handkerchief from her sleeve blew her nose. She held it, crumpled, in her hand. "This belonged to Lily. I took all her handkerchiefs. Louisa doesn't know that, or she'd be livid about that too."

She shook her head. "You know, it didn't start with the money, insurance. It goes back as long as I can remember."

"And you're not to feel a bit guilty about that little bit of money. Lily knew. She knew, Claire. She left you that for a reason, a good reason. And no one can say that you haven't put it to good use. Your education, your job." Naomi laughed. "Would that you would have spent some of it on a frivolous luxury or two. Which you should. A trip. Europe. You should visit Europe.

"You're way too serious, Claire. I think Louisa did that to you. Beat all the – I don't even know the word – made you sad, lonely, deep down, under all that serene front. I see that. And as soon as a man does, he'll be the one for you. That I know."

Claire looked up, started to speak, then closed her mouth.

Naomi looked at her. "What?" Claire didn't respond.

"Oh, don't do that. Now, what? What were you going to say? Spill it."

Claire looked into her glass, swirled the melting ice cubes. Naomi jumped up and grabbed the glass. "Okay, I'm filling this one back up. You have got to tell me what you were thinking about. As a way to celebrate the future."

Claire pursed her lips and, taking the glass, now half-full of bourbon and ice, no water, sat back in her chair. She exhaled, then took a gulp.

"So, here it is. Here's what I want." She sat up straight, moved to the edge of the seat. "I want to lose my virginity. It's time. I don't need to be in love; I just don't want to be a virgin anymore."

Naomi burst out laughing. "Well, honey, how long have you been holding on to that one?"

Claire, looking solemn, responded, "It's been a few years. But now I've decided that the time has come. Come and passed, really. Remember the chicken-shit man?" She laughed. "And I want someone who knows what he's doing." She looked at Naomi. "You can understand that, right?"

"Now you're not thinking that I can pimp you out, do you? And what about all your college boys who are now in their fancy business training programs? Why not one of them? And why are you thinking about all this? What is going on with you?" She watched Claire drain her glass. "And so, I'm thinking you might want some ice water from now on."

In the next months, there was no more talk of Claire's virginity or lack thereof, though Naomi did, on more than one occasion, ask about potential mates, marriage and bed, at Claire's work.

"No one. Really, there is no one. Hardly any of them like me, anyway, and they are such drudges, most of them, just going from their labs to their messy offices and throwing papers full of words at me to put into some kind of intelligible order."

"Not one? Not one you think about some times? Nobody? What kind of place is that, anyway? If you can't find a man at Hopkins, there may be no hope for you. I think you just don't look. You gotta look, Claire. When they look at you, you gotta look back. I can't believe you haven't figured that out by now.

"So, I'll ask again. Is there no one that you've looked at, even if they haven't looked at you?"

Claire stared into her glass.

"Ha!" Naomi exclaimed, "there is somebody. I knew it. Spill it. Then we can figure out next steps. First thing: you gotta look back."

"Naomi, for me to look back at this guy, I'd practically have to lay across his desk. He isn't exactly a man of the world, I guess, though he is," here she paused, "a continental, I'd say."

Naomi shook her head. "I have no idea what you are talking about. The only Continental I know is a Lincoln."

Over the next weeks, Claire started looking back. She looked back at work; she looked back when she was on the bus; she looked back when she stood in line at the bank and when she picked up her dinner orders at the Blue Jay on St. Paul Street. Then she started smiling back. In three weeks, she had been on dates with four men, three of whom she thought she'd like to see again. This *looking back* thing isn't bad, she said to herself, though she was always surprised when someone, shyly, struck up a conversation with her. Shyness. She liked that, thought that it went with sincerity. It took far too long for her to realize that shyness could be as much of an act as bravado.

"So," Naomi said at their next get-together, "is one of these the one? Who will earn the right to deflower this maiden? Or will it be the Continental?"

Claire shook her head slowly from side to side.

"I'm thinking no for the Continental. I sat at a table beside him the other morning at the coffee shop by work. He may have turned his head to look at me. But that was it. No eye contact at all. Didn't ask me to sit with him, and didn't ask to sit with me."

"Well, it's a start. Who knows how they do things in Contenentia, anyway?"

Claire laughed. "So, here are some details. I've been sleuthing, on the q.t.

"He's German, but he didn't live in Germany. Someplace like Bohemia, not Bavaria, because that's Germany, or Czechoslovakia or one of the provinces somewhere around there. He was deported, I think, or escaped, after the war. He's a DP, displaced person. He came here around 1950 or so. I don't know how old he is. You know, these down-at-heel Europeans all look middle-aged."

Naomi shook her head. "Oh, I can see it all now. So he lives in East Baltimore, with his mother, grandmother, aunts, cousins, you name it, and is supposed to marry a nice Polish girl, right? A displaced person, been through the war, and now he's at Hopkins. Success story. Doesn't talk to you, doesn't buy you a cup of coffee. And this is the one person in the whole of the hospital complex you're interested in." Naomi shook her head. "Not a doctor, not a surgeon, not a fancy professor. You want to know a DP with no money, who won't even talk to you."

"Well, you asked," Claire said, and took three cookies from the plate. "And, anyway, I'm thinking that he wouldn't be the one to deflower me, anyway. He'd be much too intense. Too Hungarian."

"Like you know from Hungarian."

With her last words, Naomi plunked her glass on the coffee table, stood up and shook herself. "Time for me to head South. I've preached enough."

Claire unwound her legs and joined her friend by the door. "You know, I've never told anybody what I've been able to share with you. About Louisa, not the virgin thing. Thank you for listening." She stopped. "Well, actually I've never told anyone about the virgin thing, either."

The friends hugged goodbye. "You need to do that Mary Martin number – only wash Louisa right out of your hair. And maybe that Continental while you're at it."

Claire turned Naomi to face the door. "Enough advice," she said, and touched the back of her head as she closed the door.

Twenty-three

It was late; it was cold; Claire was chilled to the bone, tired, just wanted to get to the safety of her apartment. But she had said she would go, something special that Naomi had cooked up, and she wasn't that far away. It had been months since they had seen one another. Naomi was "out of town," as she phrased it. Claire knew enough not to ask for details. While Claire had opened her life to Naomi, she knew, and accepted, that part of Naomi stayed hidden from her.

Maybe tonight she'll tell me, let me know what goes on with her, Claire thought. She would take the bus directly to Light Street and be there in less than thirty minutes. She wouldn't stay long; Naomi would understand.

Claire buttoned her coat, and, wishing that she hadn't worn such high heels, pulled on her leather gloves. They had been Lily's. She walked south and west to the bus stop. She had forgotten to wear a hat and the wind and cold chilled her ears, the start of a migraine, she worried. No alcohol tonight. Definitely no alcohol, regardless of whatever concoction Naomi wanted to try. She stuffed her hands in her pockets. She'd wait until she got to Naomi's to light a cigarette.

"An aspirin and a cup of tea," she breathed as Naomi came down the stairs to open the door. "And just let me sit on the couch for a second."

Tea, aspirin, cigarette dispatched, Naomi looked at her friend. "You know, you could have canceled this evening. I would have understood."

"Oh, no. I was almost here anyway at work, and just give me a minute. Then I'll be my normal ebullient self. Anyway, I have news. And you must as well. So what is this special thing you have to show me?"

"I'm thinking that we need to save that one. It's a new drink I discovered. Pink Squirrel. Isn't that the best name? But I'm not

112

drinking alone, and this is not the night for you and alcohol, I suspect. We can do it later. And by then, maybe I'll figure out another drink. Someone came into the shop last week with a pamphlet of how to make cocktails. I'm working my way through it before I put it out to sell."

Claire smiled. "You have the best attitude. I need some of that. Wave your magic wand and transfer it please." Claire shifted, sat up, then sank back against the cushions, unhooked her stockings. She stretched her feet before her, leaned in to massage her toes.

"So, do you want to hear my news? Not waiting for a response, she continued. "I have met a man. I think that he might just be the one. And he likes me. So I got this virgin thing out of the way, and I'm finding a husband at the same time."

Naomi leaned forward.

"I met him at a dinner party weeks, three, no, four weeks ago now. We sat across from one another; there were only eight of us, so we could actually talk. He's handsome, tall, dark, went to Washington and Lee, with one front tooth that just overlaps with the other. Charming, not just the tooth, I mean, but that's charming too. And now he's in one of those executive training programs you talked about, one of the insurance companies whose names I can't keep straight, INA, CNA, ABC. Who knows? And he seems interested, very interested, in me. And he is handsome, did I tell you that?

"And things are moving along, fast, very fast, if you know what I mean." Claire raised an eyebrow.

Naomi pursed her lips. "Well, I get that he's handsome and that one of your goals has been achieved. But who is he? You've told me everything about him except who he is, what he's like. Or is he simply an up-and-comer? Highly suitable? Is that what you're looking for?"

Claire bristled. "Well, I'm not looking for unsuitable, if that's what you mean, Naomi."

Both stopped, realizing that these were the first cross words that had been spoken between them. Naomi stopped, aware of what Claire wanted to hear, and what she didn't.

"Oh, pet, no. I didn't mean that at all. Sorry that it came out that way. It's just a surprise. And you're moving pretty fast, aren't you? Maybe too fast?"

Claire put her feet on the floor, looked at the wall across from her, bit her lower lip. "Really, Naomi. Really." She stopped, shook her head. "I'm sorry too. I guess it's just my head tonight. I expected you to be happy, to whoop it up, not question me. Not about this. You know how I want this, want to be happy. I need you to be behind me, to be happy for me." She balanced herself as she hooked her garters, stepped into her shoes.

"Really, I think it best if I head home, take a hot shower, another aspirin or two, and crawl into bed. Let's call this a night. What do you say?" By the time Claire had finished her sentence, she had picked up her coat.

Naomi stood, watched Claire walk to the door. "You know that I only want what's best for you, Claire. That's the only reason I said what I said."

"I think that I'm the one who can determine what's best for me. And thank you for a lovely evening." Claire opened the door. As she headed down the stairs, she turned. "And we're almost engaged. So you'd better get used to it."

Naomi decided that it was best not to go after her.

Twenty-four

He watched as she stepped onto Wolf Street. She ran toward the car and opened the passenger side door.

"So sorry. Hope you haven't been waiting long. I'm so nervous I can hardly breathe.'

He took her hand, leaned over to kiss her. "A lunch, a breather, then you'll be more than prepared. You'll knock 'em dead." He kissed her again.

"Corned beef? Jack's?" he asked, though he had already turned the car south on the way to Lombard Street.

The lunch crowd had thinned and they found a table as soon as they walked in. Their sandwiches arrived in short order. Claire cut her halves into halves. "I've been so wrapped up in myself, in this interview. But after today, I'll be myself, we can be ourselves. Really plan this wedding." She saw his expression and stopped short. She felt herself slowly lower her sandwich to the plate.

"What is it? What's wrong? Has something happened?"

He shifted in his chair, looked at the window to his right. "We can talk about it later."

Claire swallowed, went to pick up her water. The glass slipped from her left hand, and she grabbed it with her right before it fell over. She cleared her throat and sipped, slowly, trying to give herself time, working hard to calm herself, not appear like a nervous school girl before this man, this boy, this fiancé.

"We can talk about it now." She smiled with what she hoped was a sweet expression. "If it's important, let's talk about it now. What's happened?"

He pushed his plate to the side. "It's not a good time for this. I know that. But I've got to say this, tell you."

Claire fought a wave of nausea, felt the perspiration run down her sides, and immediately worried that it would not dry by the time of her interview. She shook her head. "What? Tell me what?"

"It's this marriage thing. I'm just not sure about this marriage thing. You, your career, you seem so sure of yourself, everything going your way, sure of the life you'll have. But that's not what I want, Claire. Married to someone important, maybe one day more important than I am. None of my friends have that kind of life. They have wives at home, waiting for them at night, children. The man is the head of the family. It's not a partnership, it's not equal. That's the life I know. That's the life I want. Can you give it to me? Can you? Do you love me enough to be my wife?"

Claire stared across the table. "Wives waiting at home? That's what you think? That's what you want? A wife waiting for you? Do I love you enough to be that?" Her words came out in a hiss. "Your question should be 'Do you love me enough?'"

She tapped the table with the index finger on her right hand. "And where do you think the men are, those nights at the office, those business meetings? Just how much do they love those wives-at-home? Oh, yes. They're happy, all right. As long as they have the freedom to do as they please, as long as they please. And certainly, no questions asked." She heard her voice come out as a croak.

"Is that what you want? What you think you want?" As she pushed her plate away, it careened into his. "And you chose now, today, this lunch, to tell me this?"

"Wait. You asked."

Claire put up her hand to stop him. She pulled a handkerchief from her purse, looked away, blinked hard. "Don't you think I think about that life sometimes? That picket fence, children? But I'm grown up enough to realize that I can't have it all. And I'm not ready to give this up. I've worked hard for this, and opportunities keep presenting themselves. Can't you see that? How stupid would it be for me to ignore this?"

She stopped, folded her hands on the table. Her outburst had startled her and she wondered if she wasn't entirely surprised, if she had ignored what she should have paid attention to.

She took a breath, felt a strength. She recognized a familiar stoicism. "I really need to get back to work now." She tilted her head to the right, lifted an eyebrow. "Would you mind?"

He signaled for the check. "Claire, I'm so sorry that I said, well, what I said, but you want me to be honest, don't you? To tell the truth?"

Claire pressed her lips together. "You know, whenever anyone asks you if you want them to tell the truth, well, that…" She didn't finish her sentence. She had run out of words, and thoughts. She took a deep breath. "Well, I can't say much for your timing. Unless you planned it this way." She stared, hard, not taking her eyes away.

"You want me to tell the truth, don't you?" He looked down at the table.

She stood. "Yes, of course. It was I. You can mark yourself blameless."

They walked to the car in silence. No words were spoken on the drive to back to Wolfe Street. When he pulled to the curb, Claire opened the door, and faced him, her arms supported by the door. She leaned in, locked eyes with him.

"You fucker." Claire savored each of the three syllables.

She slammed the door and strode into the building. She did not look back.

117

Twenty-five

They were on their second bourbon-and-water and still laughing.

"I'm so proud of myself for being such a bad influence. I can die now; my work is done." Naomi closed her eyes and brought the frosted glass to her forehead.

"I'm telling you. The words just rolled right off my tongue you should have seen his face."

"Oh, I can see his face. Those words, coming from my Mt. Holyoke, classy, educated friend. 'You fucker.' I love it."

The two laughed again. Then the room was full with silence. Claire stood, straightened a print that didn't need straightening. One of Monet's Waterlilies. She had bought it at the Museum three Sundays ago, had it framed at Bendan's. Her splurge, her gift to herself to celebrate life as a happily-single woman.

"Good to laugh, I guess. I thought," she paused, emptied her glass, remained facing the wall, "I thought it would be perfect." Naomi saw her shrug her shoulders.

"You don't have to close that door; it doesn't have to end. You can think it out, wait, see what happens."

"I've tried not to second guess myself, wonder if I should have just said that I understood, comforted him. And what does that lead to? A lifetime of me comforting him. The stage would be set.

"You know, I almost understand what he said, how he felt, feels. But to do it an hour before the biggest meeting of my life, that he chose that time, that lunch, to do that, what does that say about him?

"That's what I'm thinking these days. Better now than later, right?"

Claire turned to face her friend. Naomi was silent, waiting for Claire to answer her own question.

Claire continued. "It says a lot, I think. More than I wanted to know. That's what I'm thinking about. That, and how badly I thought I wanted to be married. Right now, I think it's not that bad, that I don't want to be married that bad, I mean, that I need to stand up for myself." She drained her glass, then stood and lit another cigarette. "Ergo, Monet," she said as she indicated the print with a wave of her left hand.

"So, I guess this means that you were right." She took a deep drag of her Lucky Strike, smiled. "At least I wasn't left at the altar. I can now say that I was dumped over a corned beef sandwich at Jack's on Lombard Street. How many people can add that to their resume of love?"

Naomi remained silent. Not the time to make light, she decided. When Claire returned to her chair, Naomi bit on her upper lip, and began.

"The way I see it, you have everything going for you. You're classy, anyone can see that. You're smart. You're educated. You have a better job, more important job, than anyone I know. Your stuff is sent all over, read by smart people. Now you have a promotion, you got that promotion even after your lunch experience. More travel, everywhere, talking about whatever it is you talk about. I'm not sure exactly why you want, wanted, to be married. But if you do, it will happen. If not to this one, there should be a line out there waiting for you.

"You can call the shots on this one. They should be out buying diamonds, flowers, for you. I'm saying you call the shots on this one."

Naomi stubbed out her cigarette and stood up. "I need to get going, leave you with your decisions." She pulled on her coat. "Call me if you need to talk. But I know you'll do the right thing, the right thing for you, Cheeky."

She walked toward the door. "Next week, my place. And, really, you need to get yourself a car."

Claire laughed, pushed her friend into the hallway. "Enough advice, enough nagging, for today." She shook her head. "What would I do without you?"

"Naomi nodded. "You got that right."

He didn't contact her. She kept the ring, though she would have returned it had he asked. She hocked it, her first visit to a pawnshop, accompanied by Naomi, who took care of the negotiations.

She used the proceeds to finance a trip to Europe, a three-week tour sponsored by the Hopkins Alumni Association.

Twenty-six

A long lunch break, she said. Some business at the bank. Claire's boss nodded his approval.

"If it runs too late, I may not be back," she added.

He nodded again, not looking up from his report.

She relaxed as she caught the bus; one transfer would take her right to the corner. She straightened her shoulders as she pulled open the brass door to the Union Trust Company, Charles Street Branch, seven minutes early for her one o'clock appointment. Walk with assurance, she told herself, and matched her stride to her will. She realized that she had been thinking about this for years now. Time to put this to rest, she thought. Time to let it go.

A tall man in a three-piece grey pin-stripe suit came to her side. "Are you Miss Mueller?" Claire nodded. "I'm Howard Ellington." He led her to his office and indicated the dark brown leather chair across from his desk. He sat behind the polished mahogany desk and looked at her expectantly.

When she didn't speak, he said in a gentle voice, "You said that you were interested in getting information about a loan?" He waited, surprised by his level of comfort with the silence.

Claire was mortified when a nervous giggle escape. She cleared her throat and spoke. "Oh, Mr. Ellington, I apologize. I'm more nervous than I anticipated. I should have rehearsed my speech."

Ellington smiled, worked to put Claire at her ease. "Don't be embarrassed. You'd be surprised. Even the most experienced of businessmen become nervous when they have to ask for money." He laughed, then recognized that the woman across his desk wasn't smiling. He tried to gauge her age, then realized that it would be on her account. He looked down at the file on his desk.

As he looked away from her, Claire began to speak.

"Yes. I would like to inquire about a loan. Two thousand dollars." She coughed, then continued. "As you can see," for she had sensed that it was a file of her account that he was looking at, "I have almost that amount in my account, my savings account." She opened her purse, searched for the navy-blue bankbook.

"I do see that," he responded. "And may I ask what the loan is for? Would this be for an automobile?"

Claire was horrified to hear another giggle escape. She placed her hand in front of her mouth. Grow up, Claire, she told herself. Act like an adult, an adult with her own apartment.

"It is for my sister," she said.

Ellington waited. "I'm afraid that I'll need a bit more information, Miss Mueller. And you can be assured that anything you say here is confidential to your account."

Claire nodded and began to talk. She found that the words flowed, no tears. She heard herself going back to her childhood, telling this man of the beatings that Louisa administered, knowing that she would not be punished, of cutting remarks and humiliations administered, of Lily's death and learning of the insurance policy, of Fritz's encouragement to keep the money, not to share it, of how she had used the money, of Louisa's continuing rage.

"I just feel that if I give her the money, she'll leave me alone."

Claire sat back in the chair. Exhaustion was soon followed by humiliation. She put her hand to her forehead, exhaled, shook her head. "Mr. Ellington, I apologize again. I don't know what to say. I am ashamed, embarrassed." She blinked, inhaled, forced herself to meet Ellington's eyes. "I am normally so much better prepared. I am so sorry for burdening you with my personal situation. I realize that it is totally irrelevant to my request." Claire shifted in her chair, straightened her back. "Please disregard my outburst. It is not typical of me, I can assure you of that.

"I have a good job. I am a steady, steadfast employee, and I manage money well." Claire felt that she had moved outside her body, was looking at a vision of how to request a loan.

The banker had remained silent during Claire's words. "Miss Mueller, I know I am out of order here, and I apologize in advance. But do you think, honestly, that giving your sister this money will change things?

"I know that it is not my place, and your credit history is good so that there will not be a problem with the loan, but may I ask that you take a while, a few days, at least, to reconsider. Are there other family members you can consult?"

Claire held on to her purse in her lap. "Yes. I appreciate your advice. I didn't realize I was as emotional about it as I obviously am. One should never undertake a major decision unless it is in a calm, rational manner." As she said these words, Claire felt that she was on stage, observing herself. She stood, reached to shake Ellington's hand.

"Please be in touch, Miss Mueller. Either way, though I think you have nothing to worry about. If you decide that you want this loan, that is."

Claire smiled; her face flushed, not only from embarrassment.

Ellington came from behind his desk. "Let me walk you to the door."

When they reached the entrance, they shook hands again. He cleared his throat. "Would you allow me to take you to lunch sometime?" He paused. "Regardless of your decision, of course."

Claire looked down, was aware that her heart was racing. "I'd like that. Yes. I'd like that very much."

She turned and walked to the bus stop on St. Paul Street. As she waited, she reached into her purse, pulled out a cigarette, and lit it. I need this, she thought, regardless of who might see me smoking on the street.

And of course, he called, and of course he was married. And of course, they met for lunch the next day. The Chesapeake, on Charles Street. Around two p.m. he called the bank to say that his meeting was taking longer than expected and that, most likely, he would not be able to get back to the office that day. At 2:30 p.m. she called the school and said that something personal had come up and that she would see them tomorrow morning.

The lunch continued, a second martini for both, which both knew was the signal. Claire laughed, leaned back in her chair and laughed again, and felt not a bit tipsy. Ellington felt his heart melt. Yes, he thought, that is exactly the right expression. As he smiled, he felt his heart melt, his eyes fill. This is it, he thought, really it.

At five p.m., they noticed the waiters laying the tables around them with fresh linen. Claire feigned a gasp when she looked at her watch, though she knew they had been there for hours. "I cannot believe this. We really must say that lunch is over." She looked at Ellington, laughed again. "Well, this has been fun."

He didn't speak. "Let me drive you home, at least." He bit his lip as he spoke.

"I don't think so. I think bus fumes are just what I need right now." She rose to go, grateful that she could walk without a hint of a stagger, or so she thought. It was not what the waiters observed.

The pair walked to the door. "May I call you?" he asked.

She smiled and looked at her feet. "You know the answer to that."

She turned and walked toward the bus stop at the corner. She didn't turn around, but waved her fingers goodbye. Ellington clicked his heels and headed back to the bank.

Twenty-five minutes later she threw her purse on the floor as she entered her apartment. Walking into the bedroom, she took off her girdle, stockings still attached. Unbuttoning her skirt, she lay on top of the bed, closed her eyes, smiled.

Oh, love, she thought. Again. And married. She put her hand to her mouth, bit down on her thumb. He will call again, soon. That she knew.

And so, he did. That night, in fact, before midnight. Claire stumbled from her bed to the phone in the living room. She knew who it would be.

"I just had to hear your voice."

She didn't respond.

"Are you there? I can't stop thinking about today. I close my eyes and all I see is you. I can't..."

She stopped him. "Don't. Not now. Really, not now."

"Can I see you again? I don't think I could stand it if you said no."

She nodded, but could not bring herself to speak. "It would be better if you called me at work. For now," she said and shook her head as she said it.

"Tomorrow, then. Tomorrow."

She hung up the phone without replying and walked back into the bedroom.

She was ready when he called, had her professional-woman voice and demeanor prepared.

"Howard, I'm not saying this because I am a moral person, or because I don't want to hurt your wife or your family. I'm entirely selfish. I'm saying this just for me, to protect me, to do what is best for me.

"So, you know what I'm about to say. It could have been wonderful for us, I think, at least that's how it plays out in my fantasy. But life isn't a fantasy, and I will be the one to be hurt the most. You might be, but you will go home to your family and then

125

settle back in your routine, and, just perhaps, only you will be the wiser. But I will bear the lingering hurt. It's on me.

"You have been a wonderful friend, and I thank you for the times, or really, the time, that we've spent together. But this will not work. I think we both know that. So, now I hang up while I still have at least some dignity."

He started to speak, but she hung up before she could make out his words.

Well, that's over, she thought.

But of course, it wasn't. And of course, she was the one who was hurt the most.

And no, she didn't ask for the loan, and no, she didn't give the money to Louisa.

Twenty-seven

Claire gathered her papers and walked to the office at the end of the hall. At first glance it looked empty, desk cleared of all but one medium stack of papers, file folders placed in a metal rack, no one sitting at the desk. She tapped lightly on the doorframe as she walked in, prepared to leave a note on the desk. To her left she saw Viktor, standing in the middle of a crush of scattered papers, his eyes closed. She cleared her throat. "Oh, I hope that I'm not disturbing you. I believe that we had this time down to meet. To discuss your proposal."

Viktor opened his eyes. "I heard you. I was trying to complete my thought."

Claire felt her head cock to the side. She was silent, trying to decide how to respond. Was he rude? Was he asocial? He looked at her like he had never seen her before. The Continental. What would Naomi say?

Shoulders back, show confidence, she told herself. "Well, would you like me to come back? Would you want to reschedule, sometime later today? We do need to start in on this if we're to meet the deadline."

Viktor walked to his desk. Unapologetic, he spoke. "Please. Sit. We can work. I have read over your initial scribbles."

Claire sat, puzzling how to best proceed. "Yes. It was a bit of a challenge, I must say. But I think that I got the gist of it. What are your thoughts?"

Viktor sat straight. "Of course, I must be honest. You do want that, am I correct?"

Oh god, Claire thought, not another 'you want me to be honest'.

Not waiting for a response, he continued. "So. To me it reads like the work of a kindergarten student. Not at all what I would want, how I want my work to be presented. Surely you can do better. Or perhaps it is best if it is submitted exactly as I forwarded it to the Dean. These are not ignorant people; they will know what

I am proposing, without having it so-called translated by a non-scientist. I sure you can see my point, Miss..." Viktor paused. Claire did not help him by supplying her name.

Silently thankful that she had worn her best suit, red with one silver button at the waist, Claire sat erect. "Viktor," she started, purposely using his first name, "this is not at all an indictment of your work, your style of writing. In fact, it is a model for scientific work. I recognize that, of course. And were the proposal going to scientists only, it would be presented exactly as you have written it. But, fortunately or unfortunately, there are others at this foundation who will be making the final decision. And they need to, want to, know exactly what they are voting on. That's my job. That's what I do. I take scientific jargon, if you will, and translate it so that it is understandable to an educated, albeit non-scientific, jury.

"And denigrating my work by calling it 'kindergarten' benefits no one. I'm sure that you can appreciate that. In fact, I find it quite insulting." Claire wondered where this courage to speak her mind came from, and worried that it would not last throughout this session with this arrogant foreigner. Just who does he think he is, she asked herself, this guy who comes to this country and now deigns to judge how I write. What a jerk. Just another jerk. And to think, I told Naomi that he was interesting, that he was the only man here that just may be of interest to me.

Viktor pursed his lips. "Yes, you are right. Your version. Well, I was insulted as well, what you did to my work."

Claire felt her heart beat. How to hold on to the person she had presented herself as. She exhaled. "So." Uncomfortable with the silence, she raced to fill it. "So," she paused. "Now that I reconsider, perhaps it would have been better had we met to discuss this before I prepared my version. I thought that this way would save time, but now I see that it was, well, injudicious. Because we haven't formally met. Before this, I mean."

Viktor maintained his silence, satisfied that he was making this secretary-with-power squirm. He would ask about her, find someone who might know her. And really, someone, a woman no less, rewriting his work. This America. Arrogance everywhere.

Claire stood. "So." I must stop saying 'so,' she decided. "Would you like to discuss this further? A version of what I sent you will accompany your original work. And the deadline is closing in on us. If you could be specific, identify exactly where, what, you found 'kindergarten-like' in my adaptation, I would be happy to discuss it with you. We obviously have more work to do on this, and it would be advantageous that we approach it with at least a modicum of self-respect, mutual-respect, I mean." God, thought Claire, where is this coming from? One would think that I had self-confidence. She smiled, then realized that the smile was on her face, not just in her mind.

Viktor stood behind his desk, his smile matching hers. Claire had no way of knowing that Viktor didn't smile often. He didn't smile at all. "Yes," he said. "At least of modicum of mutual respect. Maybe outside the office. Over coffee. In the first-floor coffee shop?"

"I can do 3:00 this afternoon. Would that fit?"

Viktor walked to the side of his office, bent down to pick up the papers strewn on the floor. "Yes. There. Then. Thank you. Miss…ah, would you tell me your name again."

Claire bit her lip. He really didn't know her name. No hope. "It's Mueller. Claire Mueller." She turned and left his office. "And please bring my version and your notes," she added, without turning around. Another fucker, she thought, surprised at how easily the word came to her.

Viktor walked to his desk, sat on the edge, and smiled.

Twenty-eight

Fritz lingered over his cigarette and coffee. He looked around Claire's dining room. "You've done an exemplary job here, Claire. Really, it's homey, but also, ah, what's the word? Sophisticated, I think. You have your mother's touch, I think."

Claire smiled. Compliments from Fritz were frequent; comparisons to Lily, rare. "Thanks to your contributions, you know. I'm hoping that I've inherited your eye as well." The rug, his subtle suggestions about placement of chairs, end tables, a slight shift from the rectangular, these were cues from Fritz. Claire saw the difference only after she had made them. She feared that she had neither his eye nor her mother's taste. Following what others suggest, that's what I'm good at, she thought, and wondered if that were to be her lot in life.

Her job, her career, she wasn't sure how much, if any, thought, internal direction, she had given to it. She was a hard worker; she believed that she had good common sense. That, and a large vocabulary. Common sense, an ability to speak as if she were smarter than she knew she was. And here she sat, entertaining her stylish, urbane father, in her own apartment, paid for with her own salary. No husband, no fiancé, no boyfriend. Just Claire, with her own furniture. Not even a cat.

But she did know how to cook three recipes that belied her disinterest in cooking, enough for the minimal entertaining that she did. And Fritz thought anything she managed to put on the table a feast. Sometimes it came from the Blue Jay across the street. That didn't matter. For the them, it was the company. They could, and did, talk about anything, books, work, plays, movies, television programs. They did not talk about Louisa. Ever. Both thought that it better that way. Calmer, more peaceful. And what remained to be said, anyway?

The two moved to the living room, Claire to her favorite chair, reupholstered since its days at Sylvan Cliffs, Fritz to the sofa, where he put his stockinged feet on the tufted leather ottoman, a recent birthday gift, from him, to Claire. She brought over two highball glasses, a quarter filled with bourbon, the cut glass tumblers also a gift from Fritz.

"There is a fellow at work, I think you would like him. I think the two of you would get on. He's an odd guy, but one that I think you would like. A DP. From Prague. He's a biologist by education, a Ph.D., not a medical doctor. But he's done lots of interesting research, and I'm rewriting a few of his articles for publication in some trade scientific mags. He's quiet, but I think there's a lot in there."

Fritz looked up. This was the first time Claire had mentioned anyone from her work, the first time she had mentioned anyone since her fiancé debacle. Odd, he thought, but good. Maybe she was making friends there. "Of course. Arrange it. What's the name? And when would you like to do this? Soon?"

"Well, I'm seeing him almost every day now. He has several proposals, articles in progress. So I'll bring it up on Monday, get a few times that work for him, then I'll call and we can work it out. I think it would be best if we came to your place. It's more," Claire hesitated, "manly." She laughed as she thought of the word.

Fritz looked over at Claire, paused before he spoke. "And this manly Czech, is he someone that …" He left the rest of his sentence unfinished.

"Oh, no, Faht. Nothing like that. He's just, well, not even a friend, I'd say. And he's not Czech. He's German, one of those Ethnic Germans who lived there. There's something about him that reminds me of you, although he is one of the most socially awkward people I've ever met. Sort of a gloomy Gus. But there is something there that I like. Not as a suitor, though. Never that. Just friendly like."

"And this friendly-like guy's name is?"

"It's Viktor. Viktor Kreis."

131

Twenty-nine

Claire watched from her window as Viktor parked his car on 31st Street. Lucky to find a close spot, she thought, and went to the door to open it. Viktor tapped lightly before he entered, then went to embrace Claire who stood still, stiff. He didn't understand why; neither did she.

"What do you say that we walk over to Faht's? You have such a good parking spot, and the weather isn't bad."

"You are becoming European," he answered. "Not getting in your car to drive a few blocks, like most of them." He smiled, then added, "Not that that is wrong, mind you. Just American."

"You are rubbing off on me, perhaps," Claire responded, "and, like a European, I don't own a car. She walked toward the living room. "Would you like one for the road?"

Viktor shook his head. "I'd prefer to keep a clear head tonight, I think, meeting this famous Fritz."

Claire smiled, and pulled on her coat. "Let's head out. And it will be fine. You'll like him, I think."

The streetlights came on as the pair crossed Charles Street, and the sky had darkened by the time they reached Ambassador Apartments. Fritz had the door open, and standing up from his chair when they arrived, greeted them warmly. He has a firm handshake, Fritz thought, and winked his approval to Claire as the couple settled in.

Fritz fixed the drinks, bourbon and water for the three, as Claire and Viktor settled on separate ends of the couch. He asked about Viktor's job, an easy segue, he thought, into finding out what makes this man tick, why his daughter seems to think him special, special enough to bring him around to meet her father.

Claire watched the two, more than surprised at Viktor's apparent ease with Fritz. He was relaxed, she realized, a facet that she rarely saw when he was with others. She thought of him as a tightly-wound spring, and realized how nervous that made her much of the time. At first, when they were together, it took a

132

while, five, ten minutes for them to become comfortable with one another. Now, she thought, a trace remained, one that disappeared after the first touch, always his, Viktor becoming himself, at ease with himself. But here, with Fritz, that seemed to come right away.

She started when she heard Fritz ask about his war experiences. She had specifically asked him not to do this, not to pressure Viktor to talk about things that he obviously didn't want to share. Viktor had told her that he wanted to leave all that behind him, concentrate on his life now. She had never delved into his past. Claire pushed back into the soft sofa cushions. This will not go well, she thought, this evening that she had wanted to work. Then she heard Viktor's voice; he was talking, confiding in Fritz, as if she weren't present.

"My parents were German, ethnic Germans they called us, though both sides had been in Czechoslovakia for generations, before it was even Czechoslovakia, when it was Bohemia. So I always knew that I was German, also Czech, but better, you see. Ridiculous, but there you have it. I don't think it mattered much to me. I was young; it was all I knew.

"My parents were quite elderly when I was born. I am an only child. So, I went to the regular school, although most Germans went to their own schools. I spoke German and Czech, then we learned other languages in school. Not English, unfortunately. That came later, and I think it is never the same when one learns a language as an adult. So forgive the slights I use, yes?"

Fritz nodded, a signal for Viktor to continue. "And the war? How was that for you?" Claire closed her eyes. Why was Fritz doing this, she asked herself.

"So, I was young, of course. My father had a dry-cleaning business, not wealthy at all, but enough. We lived over the shop; an apartment, but large, spacious. House-proud I think they were, now that I remember it. And for a while, everything was as normal for me, for my child eyes, my friends' eyes. Then my mother kept me home from school. At first, I liked it. We had books, and she would quiz me about what I had read. Then I had to stay away from the windows. That was when I realized some of what had

133

been going on around me. I was a very naïve boy, teenager. I see that now. Stupid I was. So it came to me quickly, like lightning, I think. Things started happening, escalating, I think the word is. I saw that my mother was keeping, the word is hoarding, yes? hoarding food, but not cooking it. So we were always just a bit hungry, always, and that made us snap at one another. That and being so close together all the time. My father had closed the shop by this time, and I realized that it had been targeted, though I cannot tell you to this day by whom, or by what group. By that time, everyone seemed to hate one another. No one trusted. As morass, I think the word.

"We had run out of matches, so my father went out to see if he could find any. So. That is the last time either my mother or I saw him. The next day she went to look for him. She told me to stay in the house, to not go near the window. And. That was the last time I saw her."

Claire realized that she had been holding her breath when she heard the sound of her own gasp. Viktor looked over at her. "Ah, too much, yes? So we can discuss other things?" Claire went into the kitchen to arrange a plate of cheese and sausages, and placed a wet napkin on her cheeks. She could feel the heat through the cloth.

When she returned to the living room, Viktor was seated, elbows on his knees, his hands over his eyes. But he was talking, talking to Fritz.

"The Nazis, the war ending, everyone hated the Germans. Even those who had no problem with them before, as long as they were harassing someone they didn't like. So I knew that to be German was not something I wanted people to know. Everyone was leaving, rushing around, chaos. I went out into the street, started walking with everyone else. I kept quiet; there was no one I knew. I put on three layers of clothes before I went out of the house. I don't know how I knew to do that. Maybe I saw other people in the street with all those clothes on, even though it was Spring. I don't know, and I can't even tell you how many days, or where, or when that was. I do remember the hunger, though. I should have taken food with me, but I didn't think of it.

"And the smells. Rotting corpses. And we even got used to that; we just stepped over them. They meant nothing. I had no idea where I was walking. Like a dream, *Traum*, *Albtraum*, nightmare, only you are not asleep. You are not awake either. Just present somehow. And not feeling anything, not even thinking, just doing.

"We were on the road and a truck came by, and the soldiers loaded women and children into the back of it. I didn't even look up. Then I felt myself being lifted by the collar and one of them, the soldier, pulled me into the front beside him. So if you believe in angels, he was mine. I have no idea why he chose me. Maybe I reminded him of someone, perhaps himself. American. He was American. He asked me my name. I told him, and said that I was Czech. No English of course. But I guess he understood."

Claire tried to pass the plate of cheeses. Fritz gave a slight shake of his head, then nodded to Viktor.

"Surely this is boring to you. This story."

Fritz leaned toward Viktor. "I want to hear you, your story. Perhaps you need to tell it."

Viktor shook his head. The silence in the room hung heavy. He picked up his glass, drank, looked over at Claire.

"Well, I continue. But you tell me when there is enough, too much, I think. These old memories." Claire sat tall in her seat, knees clamped together. Fritz pursed his lips, put his head to one side; Viktor exhaled.

Fritz rose to freshen their drinks, spoke with his back to the room. "We are imagining the unimaginable. And you lived it. I was there, the first war, the Great War they called it. But America never saw it, even when we were there. The English, the Germans. They tasted war, I suppose. We only witnessed. A difference."

Handing them their glasses, he leaned down to spear a square of salami. "And now all is back to normal for the world, I suppose. And how does one, how does a country, a world, get back to normal?" He paused. "How did you get back to normal?"

135

Claire clenched her jaw, closed her eyes. Oh, Faht, she said to herself, leave this alone. Leave him alone. Didn't you hear what I told you before. He doesn't talk about it. Don't ask him. He doesn't talk about it.

Her eyes flew open at the sound of Viktor's voice. "I ended up in Regensburg, somehow with the Poles, Ukrainians. And they hated the Germans. So I let them think I was Czech. We all look the same. Ridiculous it is, all this hate. Mainly I kept quiet, listened. Chaos all around. People coming, going, no sense of anything.

"Finally, they organized some kind of school. And they thought I was smart, so they told me to teach. And I taught from whatever books they handed me. And all I did was figure out how to get higher on the resettlement list. That was a nasty business. Now I understand better, but I saw people beaten, denounced, accused, who knows how, where, they ended up, just so someone could get one step closer to being resettled. That's what they called it. For those, like me, who didn't care where they ended up, it was easier, or harder, depending on who you talked to. Nobody knew anything. Everything was just words. To believe, well, that was not smart.

"I had told one of the ladies in the grey uniforms that I was Catholic. I was nothing, but I thought that it might get me a better bed, food. You know, if you were alive, you were a liar. Lies seemed no price to pay for an extra piece of rye bread, so.

"And that lie paid off for me somehow. I learned that I had a sponsor in the US. I left camp the next morning. I had what I wore and an Army uniform that somehow had ended up in my barracks. A truck transport to Bremerhaven, then an American troop ship. First time, and last, I hope, on a ship. Finally, we docked at the Brooklyn Navy Yards and the ladies in blue uniforms gave us three one-dollar bills.

"I simply stood there, looking a fool. We all just stood there, like ignorant baboons. Then the uniform ladies took us and somehow paired us with our sponsors. By that time, I spoke some English, though I had a difficult time understanding. Reading, I could do. The talking, that was painful to listen to. Mine and theirs. But, you see, another angel. The ride to Baltimore, a room of my own. A third angel for me to go to Hopkins.

"Why me? Why not me? Why anything? So, I just work now to try to figure out disease before another war figures out a way to destroy us all." Viktor stopped, surprised that he was out of breath.

"Mr. Mueller, please forgive me, my ramblings. I think it best not to speak of such things."

"First, call me Fritz. Second, you have given me a gift, Viktor. Knowledge, some understanding of what life was, is, like for those, well, those who experience, experienced, life so different from ours. I'm sure you must view us as spoiled, indolent." Fritz stopped, thoughtful.

"No. Not that. I just see Americans as lucky, and unaware that they are that. They think they deserve this life. That is my view. As an outsider, of course. But I am also gratified by their generosity, and I am an underserving recipient of it. I do recognize that, of course. And grateful that I am here, no longer in Prague, and away from the Russians.

"And now you have your royalty, American royalty. The young president with his American teeth and a beautiful wife, children, fit for a magazine cover, no? Glamourous. But there is a darkness in the country, I think, underneath, that no one acknowledges. If it is not spoken of, then it can't exist, not in America, yes? Fairy tale America.

"But then I am European, Eastern European. We think that there is only a dark side."

The three sat with a vague tension, silent.

"I have spoken out of turn, I think. Please accept my apologies. I do not want to spoil such an evening, such a first meeting with you."

Finally, Fritz cleared his throat. "You have given us much to think about, to consider, and I thank you for your courage, your candor. I hope that we will be able to continue our dialogue, Viktor."

The couple knew that this was their cue to rise, make their farewells. Fritz and Viktor shook hands; Claire kissed Fritz's cheek.

They said little as they walked back to Claire's apartment. "Tonight was something, Viktor. Thank you." She knew not to prolong the conversation.

Viktor did not reply, but she felt him squeeze her hand.

He kissed her when they reached her door. "I'd like to stay. Tonight, I'd like to stay."

"You'll need to move your car. They'll ticket you."

He reached for her. "I don't care." She took his hand and led him to her bed.

Thirty

Claire waited three days before she called Fritz. She wanted to sound casual, unconcerned, separate from whatever he might say. She wanted Fritz to like Viktor, and realized that this meant more to her than she wanted it to. And Viktor, how delighted she had been when she recognized that he liked, actually liked, Fritz. They had talked, Viktor had talked, openly, about his life. He had never done so with her. She had accepted that part of his history was closed to her. And, she admitted to herself, she was a bit, more than a bit, jealous.

Fritz sat back in his chair as he picked up the phone, looked out the window onto University Parkway, studied the reflection of the string of red lights that bounced off the wet macadam. "I was hoping that it was you." He shook the ice in his drink, waiting for Claire to begin.

"So, what do you think? He is a smart one, isn't he? I knew that you two would get along. I told him that when I convinced him that you two needed to meet." Claire realized that she was rambling, uneasy. She forced herself to stop talking, to give Fritz a chance to respond.

"Oh, I did like him. An interesting character, I'd say. Much background there, Claire, much different from, well, from us and..." Fritz stopped, considered what he wanted to say.

There was an unaccustomed silence between the two; both recognized it.

Claire heard her voice, breathy with nerves. "So, what do you think? He is a good one to have as a friend?" She hated that her last sentence came out as a question. She sounded like a child wanting her father's approval. This, she thought, was definitely not the case. Though it was.

"Are you asking for my approval, Clairedelune?" Fritz tried to keep his tone light. "So, he is a friend? Simply a friend, nothing more? You two just work together?"

"Oh, Faht, don't make this more than it is. He is engaged, to someone from his neighborhood, I think. Someone who, well, there is a lot of old-country there, the people he knows, he lives with. She's American, I think, but very connected with her family, those kinds of values. Very different from me, from the people he works with. I think that's part of why he's lonely, why we became friends. And that's all we are. Really."

Fritz closed his eyes, considered what to say next. "Well, he is certainly that. He obviously feels comfortable with you, Claire, and that's not something that comes easily to him. But I would be a bit wary. That is, if you are asking for advice. Which you are not.

"I think he's damaged, not in a way that he can help, but those war years, after the war, I think they left pretty deep wounds. And he's alone, Claire, foreign, living, making his way in a country that is not his. So much different, though I would guess that Hopkins would be a place where it would be almost comfortable to be different."

Claire thought about her own situation there, where it was definitely not comfortable to be different. She lit another cigarette before she spoke. "I know," she said, her voice soft.

Fritz picked up on her tone. "And, with all his stoicism, that fatalistic façade, he's vulnerable, Claire." Fritz cleared his throat. "You both are."

His last words hung in the air.

Claire broke this silence. "Oh, I don't know. I think not, Faht. His life is so separate; his work, his personal life, his friends from work. I think he is pretty solid."

Fritz shook his head, though Claire could not see. "Well, you're an adult, and you know him better than I." He paused. "So, I'll stop with the advice."

"He said that he'd like us, the three of us, to go out to dinner soon. His treat. So you must have made quite an impression," Claire said. "I'll be back in touch, maybe sometime this weekend."

140

She hesitated before she spoke again. "And, Faht, thank you. You know that I always listen to what you think, what you have to say. I'll think about it, I promise."

Thirty-one

It was time, she thought, to get a car. She pulled out the yellow legal pad, the mechanical pencil she used at work. She liked that the point was always sharp. A small car, easy to park. She'd have to rent a garage space. First, she'd get to that first.

1) check availability of garage space.

No need to go further until that was taken care of. No space, no car. She was not going to put herself through the misery of searching for a space on St. Paul Street, or Charles, or Calvert, or those narrow side streets. And she would still take the bus to work.

She stopped, laid her pen down. Then why do I want a car? she asked herself. She had continued to renew her license, but she wasn't sure why. While she was happy on a bus, there were those difficult times when it was too late, too far, then all the bother of calling, waiting for, a cab, regardless of the cost involved, which she secretly felt to be an extravagance. Most times friends insisted on picking her up, and she felt discomfited that she could not reciprocate. And then there was the freedom to arrive and leave at will, not to have to consider anyone's timetable but her own, not to have to work around a bus schedule. Convenience, independence, but mainly independence.

She picked up her pen again, convinced.

2) a used car, not too many miles
3) in good condition

I'll talk to Faht. He'll be delighted, she thought.

Three days later, first on the waiting list for a space in the apartment building's wooden garage in the alley, and the super said one tenant was leaving at the end of the month, she was the proud owner of a 1956 Ford Fairlane, two-toned Fiesta Red and Colonial White, partially financed through Union Trust. Ellington had moved up from the ranks of lowly Vice President, loan officer, but he had made a call for her, and when she stopped in, sitting in the same office, same chair, different loan officer, where they had met, all that was needed was her signature.

142

Transaction completed, Claire pulled on her white gloves, buttoned the pearl button at the wrist, walked the three blocks to Guilford Avenue, and took the bus back to Wolfe Street. When she arrived at her office, her coworkers gathered. A cake topped with a red sportscar sat in the break room.

Her eyes filled with tears. Without removing her coat, she began to cut slices for those gathered. "I never expected this. Really. Thank you so much." She stopped, swallowed. "This means, well, thank you."

Almost all in the group laughed, clapped. "What will the Baltimore Transit Company do now? They'll have lost their best customer," one said.

Claire looked up, shook her head. "Oh, no, I'm not sure of that at all. But I do know every one of their routes, and most of the schedules."

When she was finally alone in her office, cake, paper plates, forks dispatched, she found her face wet with tears. She couldn't quite figure out why.

Thirty-two

Dear Claire,

I don't write many letters. Really, I don't write any letters, but for you, I make an exception.

And so I'm writing this to tell you goodbye, that you have been a friend like I've never had before, not even in books. I never imagined that I would ever meet someone like you, much less be part of her life. Because that is what I believe-that I really was a part of your life – you were-and are – part of mine. I think that you have been my only true friend, apart from the librarians at the Hagerstown Library who also opened up a world to me that too I never imagined.

All this hearts and flowers – enough. I'm counting on you knowing what I'm trying to say and how I feel.

Now for some facts – a few, not all. It is best that you don't know all. Now that is too dramatic. My situation is not dire, so do not worry about that. It is just more complicated than I can figure out right now, and you know that I'm very good at figuring things out. So, this is a conundrum for me, and, after much thought and plotting and planning, all of which came to a conclusion I was not happy about, I think it is time to move on. I think the term is "reinvent myself"- and I think that I can do that.

I've left the shop, and my apartment. I packed as much as I could manage to take on my own. I've left a key for you – it's in the bottom of the mailbox – the second in from the doorway, by the stairs – you'll have to reach way down for it and finagle the way to the slot – if you can't get to it, there's no harm done. And if you can, anything

144

that you want is yours. You'll have time – though I did shut off the electricity and the gas and the phone – in the store and the apartment. I've paid up, so am leaving no debts except the mortgage and the bank can figure that out. I attribute my upstandedness to your good influence. You've made me a better person, Claire. That I know. I hope I have made you a freer one.

You are the hardest part of my life to leave. But after I get settled, maybe – or maybe not. I'm not one to hold onto the past. Doesn't the bible say something about seasons, moving on? Or maybe that was a song I heard sometime.

Of course you know that I wish you the best. Don't be sad, or hurt, or sorry that I didn't tell you before you left, or before I left. You know that's just not my way. And when I read about you in the papers for some great contribution to mankind, I'll say that I knew you when. And that you were the best friend a body could ever have.

So, I think I've said it all.

Naomi

p.s. I'm thinking what my new name will be. Haven't decided yet.

Claire sat with the letter. She'd been busy, traveling, a conference in Paris, a presentation in Bogota. She was concentrating on her career, relishing the attention and the smatterings of polite applause. When she had thought about Naomi, she told herself that she would call, later, after things quieted down a bit, when she had time. She always thought that there would be time.

She stared across the room, unseeing. A Dear John letter, she thought. Another Dear John letter. But it wasn't. That would be

145

bad, she acknowledged, but this, this letter, this farewell, this was worse. Somehow, she thought, no matter how much you loved a man, no matter how much you thought you knew him, trusted him, it was never quite a surprise to be betrayed. But this, this was different.

Not betrayal, but a goodbye. Claire sat with that, the understanding and the ache. Understanding didn't make it hurt less.

"Oh, Naomi," she said aloud, "godspeed." She smiled at her use of the phrase. Naomi would laugh if she had been there to hear Claire, would ask her whatever book that came from. But godspeed was what she felt.

Claire rose, poured herself a finger of bourbon. She used the cut-glass tumbler, added four ice cubes and left the metal tray in the sink. Then she added bourbon to the rim. She moved to the mahogany table. Naomi in some kind of trouble. Claire acknowledged to herself that she was not surprised. Naomi's businesses, her antique-junk shop, never generated enough income to support her. Claire knew that Naomi watched her money, but there always seemed to be enough, for dinners out, for movies, for shows at Ford's, the Morris Mechanic. Exactly where it came from Claire never knew, and knew that she did not want to know. For all their closeness, for all that they knew of one another's dreams and sorrows, this was an area that was, by tacit agreement, never explored.

Claire assumed it had something to do with drugs, marijuana, nothing more, she hoped. Naomi always offered weed on those weeks when Claire visited. Most times she accepted. She liked the buzz, and it didn't come with the migraine headache that more than one Manhattan brought. Claire knew that she would pay the price for what she would consume this night, but she felt unable to face the evening with clear thoughts, feelings. Not tonight. No thinking tonight.

So most likely that was it, Claire told herself, a step beyond grass that Naomi made or someone wanted her to make, or the cop on the beat ratcheting up his weekly take.

146

But, Claire thought, as she blew a perfect smoke ring, Naomi, that is who you are, and you will land on your feet, and get in touch with me, and tell your stories, and we will laugh like old times. She considered a second bourbon, then turned on the television and thought about Naomi.

The next day she called into work and took a sick day. And didn't get out of bed until afternoon.

Thirty-three

Claire held the receiver between her thumb and forefinger, turned it slowly in her hand before she placed it in its cradle. A date, a weeknight date. At least that was how she interpreted it when he asked. Now, suddenly, she wondered.

They did not have what she once would have classified as *dates*, rather they met for dinners, after work. He would call on her extension and ask if she were free that night, happy if she could make it, content if she could not. Coffee sometimes, in the cafeteria, but only if they happened to bump into one another there, no planned lunches. Both were discreet, though they would deny that the intention ever crossed their minds. He called on the weekends, always, to chat, about books, articles either had seen, noted in the Sunday *New York Times*, which both had delivered to their homes, the bulk on Saturday evenings. Then the Sunday afternoons, museums, concerts, followed by dinner cooked by Claire, dishes washed by Viktor, he laughing as she tied her apron around his waist. Then Saturday afternoons, and nights. It started with a friendly kiss goodbye after an exhilarating afternoon; then the goodbyes lingered. Encounters evolved into embraces, longer, closer each time. And then more. And more. Both recognized what was happening. Neither spoke of it. To anyone.

But to schedule a time, a weeknight, without a concert or performance to follow, never. Or at least not until today. And he had suggested meeting at Jennings Cafe, an old favorite, an out-of-the-way bar that served crab cakes that both declared Baltimore's best. Separate cars.

Too many out-of-the-ordinary things. It made Claire nervous, a knot in her stomach that remained throughout the following day and into the evening as she drove to Catonsville, a traffic-laden forty-five-minute journey from Orleans Street to Frederick Road.

Claire looked for Viktor's car in the parking lot, and when she didn't see it, hoped that he had parked on the street. She didn't want to get there first, didn't want to be the one waiting. She had thought of nothing else from the time of his call, chiding herself all the while. They were friends, good friends, but still, only

148

friends. Why should his setting up a dinner meeting cause her such upset? After all, you can't break up with a friend, can you? She knew Viktor was engaged; he had revealed that early on, perhaps during one of their first work sessions. Or had she heard it through the coffee pot grapevine? Claire worked to remember. Had Viktor ever actually mentioned his fiancé? Did she I even know her name? Her existence was not part of their conversations. No, their relationship was based on mutual interests, non-scientific ones to be sure, and their friendship was, well, different. The sex was different as well, she reasoned, based on respect, undergirded by lust, but not love. No. Both knew that that would never do. Not in the cards. So, Claire pondered, what is going on with me? Why have I felt queasy all day? Why am I nervous?

Viktor had yet to arrive as Claire entered through the back door. But the hostess recognized her, smiled, and led her to the table toward the front where they seemed to always sit.

"Expecting your friend?" she asked, and set the table for two. Claire nodded and ordered a Manhattan, this time with ice. "Lots of ice, please. And a glass of water while I'm waiting."

As Claire rearranged the silverware a second time, she saw Viktor open the main door. He looked toward the table they normally occupied, and Claire saw what she interpreted as a nervous smile cross his face. He laid his hat on the empty chair, draped his coat over it.

"I wanted to be here first, to get your drink ordered for you," he said as he slipped into the chair beside her, pulling closer to her. He smoothed her hair, and leaned in to kiss her cheek.

Claire pulled back a fraction so that his face touched the air. He straightened and looked at her. "Let us order, shall we? The regular?" And at his words the waitress appeared with Claire's drink. Viktor started to order and then smiled when the waitress completed it for him before he had a chance to finish his sentence. "Are we so boring that you know exactly what we want?" he said. Claire watched him with the waitress, thought about how often he smiled when they were together. She never saw that at work, so dour, so focused, frustrated was he. And then she wondered which one was the real Viktor.

Not waiting for Viktor's drink to arrive, she drank half the Manhattan in one swallow. "You've made me nervous, Viktor. I don't know why, but I am so nervous." Claire immediately regretted her words. Perhaps this was not the time for honesty. Perhaps there is never a time for honesty, she thought.

The second drink arrived. Viktor drank from it, no toast this evening, and put his hand on Claire's. "So. I am nervous too. I am nervous that I will lose you. I am nervous that I can even say these words, think these thoughts. And so." He stopped. Claire waited. He's getting married, she thought. He's going to tell me that he's getting married.

Viktor looked down into his drink, circled Claire's wrist with his index finger. "So. It is time, I think, that I must marry. You know about Agata, I think. I think you know about her. About us. Betrothed. An engagement of sorts. An agreement expected, arrived at with little, with no thought, no plans, never any plans, nothing specific. But now it seems to be moving with a life of its own."

Claire moved her hands into her lap, wishing that she had taken more of her drink before she did this. "Ah. Yes. So, you will marry then? You and Agata, is it?" She bit her upper lip and nodded. "And have you decided then? To do this? To do this sometime soon? Set a date, I mean."

"I should say that it appears that this has all been decided for me, for us. Her mother, you know. To whom I owe a lot, everything really. Finding me, sponsoring me, somehow finding even more sponsors for Hopkins, my education, my job, my work. It is she who is responsible for this, for me. It is what she wants, what she deserves, really. I can see that. I can. She is a wonderful woman. And this is what she always thought would be, wanted it to be, all the while she was doing all that for me.

"I had nothing, was nothing, when I arrived here. No family, no money, a rudimentary education that had prepared me for nothing. It was Lucja who saw something in me, only Lucja. And

150

then you." Viktor looked at Claire, whose eyes were focused on her lap.

Claire stretched her fingers, made a fist, extended her fingers, buying time. She smiled; her eyes fixed on the bar area across the room. "Of course. Of course, I see what you're saying. So, you must do what you consider honorable." She did not meet Viktor's gaze.

"It is soon, the end of next month. Will you attend? Will you consider it? And Fritz? I want you to be there. You are my only friends. If you could be there."

Claire nodded, then stood, awkwardly. She had not pushed her chair far back enough. She pushed the chair out with the backs of her thighs, then reached around to keep it from falling. Struggling to say the right thing, the appropriate response, she bent down to pick up her purse. "We'll be there. You know that. But I can't stay here right now, Viktor. It is too much right now. Too much for me right now. Just a bit too much."

She managed to get lost on her way home, a wrong turn onto Hilton Street. This nightmare, when will this nightmare end, she thought, as she finally recognized Washington Boulevard, miles out of her way. She pulled over, sobbing. Then, taking a deep breath, she blew her nose and headed north, home. I'll sleep in a bit, go into work an hour late she decided. I owe myself that much.

Six weeks later she stood before the mirror in her hallway. Powder blue wool sheath, light stockings, ecru heels, medium, hair in place, but a bit tousled, just the right touch of casual, she thought. She reached for her coat, the one she had bought in Paris. The blue in the tweed matched the color of her dress, almost, just the right touch of casual, and the periwinkle brought out her eyes. She picked up her purse, eggshell-colored, large enough to hold her driver's license, a handkerchief, a lipstick, and a ten-dollar bill. She wouldn't need anything else, not with Fritz by her side. Yes, she thought, just the right touch of casual, not trying too hard. The right look for today.

She stood at the corner of St. Paul and 31st Streets, an eye out for the maroon Packard that Fritz still drove. Right on time, as she knew he would be, he pulled to the curb, leaned over to open the passenger-side door for her. "You know, I thought it was your mother for a minute there. The way you stand, your posture. Lily all over again."

But not as pretty, Claire thought, and wondered if she would ever find a man who loved her as Fritz loved Lily. Maybe not, she thought, and shrugged her shoulders. Fritz looked over.

"Ready for today?"

"As ever. I'm fine, Faht, really. I'm fine." And she believed that she was.

The pair were two of only ten people on the groom's side of St. Casmir's, and she and Fritz said little as they waited for the ceremony to begin. Claire studied the flowers on the altar, at the sides of the first three rows of pews. They sat in the fifth. Claire knew that an organ was playing, but she heard nothing. She felt the rustle at the back of the church, realized that the ceremony was about to start. A moment of silence, then the *Bridal March* rang out. All stood, and she watched as Viktor, accompanied by a man she didn't know, came from the side of the church to the altar. She refused to identify the look on his face as he found her eyes.

The bride, in a dress that Claire identified as being from Etta's Bridal Shop and then chided herself for her snobbery, followed her four attendants, they dressed in blue, also from Etta's, Claire thought, on the arm of whom Claire supposed to be her father, perhaps an uncle. Claire realized that she knew nothing about this woman, only her name, that she knew more about Agata's mother. But she knew that it was not a look of wedding radiance that the bride wore. A mess, she thought, this is all a mess, then wondered why she felt nothing.

At the reception following, in the church hall, with no alcohol, Claire recognized that people assumed that she and Fritz were a couple. When the word spread that she was his daughter, she smiled as she watched women eying him. A few asked him to dance, and he dutifully, and engagingly, complied. Claire watched as Viktor and Agata had their first dance as a couple. Later, as she saw Viktor approach their table, she decided that, should he ask her to dance, she would refuse, with a demure smile that she practiced as someone brought her a plate of something she identified as being of vaguely Eastern European origin.

Viktor shook hands with Fritz, thanked him for being there for him. Claire noticed that Viktor did not say for "them." Then he turned to Claire and asked if she would take the next dance. "Take the next dance," she thought. How charmingly European. And she said yes, demurely, and held herself stiffly as he placed his arm around her waist. She realized that they had never danced.

"It's been a beautiful wedding, and Agata is a lovely bride." Claire hoped her words sounded sincere, that Viktor wouldn't recognize that her mouth, her throat, were so dry that she could barely get any words out.

"Claire. A mistake, I fear."

Claire smiled, took a step back. "Viktor, you can dance. Where did you learn to dance?"

He had no witty reply.

As they drove home, Fritz suggested that Claire come back to his apartment. "A bit of cheese, some sausages, maybe a libation. I'd like some company, I think.

"Me too. Maybe I'll spend the night, if that's okay." And she knew it would be.

Thirty-four

She dialed the number, then hung up before the first ring. He had given it to her "for emergencies." She had never called. There had been no emergences. She was not one to have emergencies. Claire tucked her legs under her; a cup of tea was by her side.

Tea, she thought. A spinster with her cup of tea. I need a cat. To make the picture complete. A spinster drinking her tea from a china cup, saucer on the lamp table, cat on her lap All I'll need then is a crocheted afghan, one made of squares from different colored yarn scraps.

She laughed to herself. "Oh, god, is this what I've become? A caricature that even I laugh at?"

She closed her eyes, remembering the bus trip home. That feeling, that familiar feeling, had arrived, Claire could pinpoint her location, at 25th and Charles. She could identify the precise location when it came upon her, close to Naomi's first store. That longing, the push, to be in her own house, her apartment, to be safe. To be safe. She heard the words in her head as she put the key in the first lock, fumbling as she aimed for the second, recently installed by the building's management, a "precautionary measure," they called it. "Absolutely no need for alarm."

Not that Claire was alarmed, she who traveled the world on her own; she who was fearless, and courageous, and strong. Just ask anyone.

She placed her hand on the receiver, then drew it back into her lap. No, she thought. Let me pull myself together. Maybe later. Maybe tomorrow. She stood up. What is wrong with me, she thought. Maybe never.

But a cat, maybe a cat, regardless of the rules. An indoor cat, Claire considered. The ones she saw from her window, too ferocious, stalking those rats in the bushes by the alley garages. How would they use the toilet?

She laughed out loud at how she thought of it. She'd ask at work. Certainly someone there had an indoor cat, all those

154

apartment dwellers, all those students. She stood and walked to her desk. On a piece of light-blue stationery, she wrote:

Cat:

Indoor
Food
Toilet
Claws
Spayed

She capped her Esterbrook pen and returned to the sofa. No need to call this evening. Maybe tomorrow. Maybe never. She smiled, realized that she felt better. Inside her apartment, safe.

And a week later, when a co-worker took a job in Manhattan, she had Oscar, a two-year-old grey tabby who was happy to find a home.

Thirty-five

She looked nice enough. She smiled; anyone would think she was one of them. She walked to the bar that was set up by the window. In the early twilight, the blooms of Sherwood Gardens could be seen, if, as she discovered, you stood at the window pressed your forehead against the glass, and, providing you knew where to look, tilted your head to the left.

Misery, she thought. Two, possibly three, hours of misery. Smiling, all that smiling, not obviously overdone, but that smile that said, "I am delighted to be here; everyone is interesting and everyone thinks I'm interesting too." Make the Manhattan last, something to hold, something to look down into when holding one's head up at a bit of an angle became just too hard.

She looked around. Surely there were those here as miserable as she. She would find them, meet their gaze, and they would get it. She would find a friend, and they would laugh about how uncomfortable they were, how they really liked the host, and his wife of course, but, really, cocktail parties. They understood misery.

Over the years, through bad examples, both her own and those of others, she had learned that using alcohol to "loosen things up" was a recipe for disaster, and she counted herself lucky that in her one experience with one-too-many (that was really two-, possibly three- too-many) she had ended up in the arms, and bed, of, as she thought of him, a stand-up guy. He looked at her with a tender fondness that morning-after, and they laughed as they showered, separately, dressed, and found the nearest White Coffee Pot for a mid-morning breakfast of black coffee and dry toast. She was, at that point, young and pretty enough that a hangover-induced migraine left her with enough spirit to laugh.

But, more's the pity, after that night, the spark was extinguished, and they remained friends, just friends, but ones who held a special type of memory. He, of course, had moved up and out, another prestigious academic institution, by the following spring. They exchanged birthday and Christmas cards, then Christmas cards, his for the last few years including a photo of his

156

ever-growing family seated, smiling, red sweaters, in front of a Christmas tree. He seemed happy, and for that, Claire was glad.

At times she wondered. The magazine articles she read told her that women love before they have sex, that women process, she thought that was the word, love and sex differently from men. But Claire, well, she certainly liked every one of the men she had slept with, or at least she did at the time, and yes, some, like Daniel, like Howard, like well, a few more, she could say she loved. And then Viktor, well, that was different.

But for her, love didn't match the lives of the women she saw around her, her friends from high school, even the few women at work. Must be Mamma's influence, she thought. Lily wasn't like other women either.

Thirty-six

"McInally couldn't find his ass with both hands and a map. But if it involves creating a chart, he's your man. Be patient. He's not stupid, just obtuse."

"Well, I thank you for that bit of advice. I've just now found out that he's my new boss."

Viktor stopped, put down his pen. A rare, and unexpected peal of laughter bubbled from his throat. "Good Jesus. You are in for it." He stopped, then smiled at her. "But so, by god, is he. I think you'll be the one to come out ahead on this one, dear Claire."

Claire sat in front of his desk, placed her folded hands on its far side. "Tell me all.," she said, then crossed her legs and leaned back in her chair. Viktor went to the door, locked it. They did not talk about work.

But McInallly wasn't the worst, or the best, boss she had. After the fourth, they blended into a mélange of ego, tortoise-shelled glasses, and wrinkled jackets in need of cleaning. The best left her alone, assigning projects and rewrites so the researchers would stay out of their offices. The worst treated her as an overpaid secretary who couldn't make a decent pot of coffee.

But her successes, her publications, always interpretations of the works of others, and duly credited, gave her a status outside the University that they acknowledged. They thought she was untouchable; she thought she would never be able to find another job if she lost this one. Both she and they took pains to conceal their respective opinions.

Thirty-seven

She recognized his voice before she saw him. A panel discussion, she, seated in the middle of the packed auditorium, close enough to see the speakers, far away enough that she could not discern their features, riffled through the conference program. She had highlighted the sessions she wanted to attend, focused on the topics, not the presenters.

Scanning the panel, she saw men, old, grey-haired, except for one. An outlier, a dark-haired man, a dark blue suit, white shirt, indistinct tie, one in from the right.

She had missed the introductions, chatting with the man seated to her left, an acquaintance from previous meetings. She concentrated on his words, trying to read his name and affiliation on his name tag that was half-covered by a fold in his brown-tweed jacket. John Somebody. Claire kept smiling, shifted in her seat hoping that it would cause him to follow and uncover that name tag.

Then. The voice. She would never forget it. She turned abruptly from her seatmate and stared straight ahead. Of course. There he was. Daniel. The same, only more handsome, she thought, his narrow face matured into what Claire now defined as craggy. She struggled to decide whether to keep looking at him or search the program for information about him.

Daniel-who-broke-my-heart. The sobriquet she gave him made her smile, remembering two children in love. He had been right, of course, sensible, for both of them. Still, she thought, and then put it out of her mind, or tried to.

Claire felt her eyes fill. John, she still hadn't learned his last name, leaned over.

"Everything all right?" he asked.

Claire nodded. This, John, she thought, looking for a conference hook-up. Well, don't we all? She turned and smiled. He might do, for later.

To an observer, casual or otherwise, she appeared to listen to the panel, firmly focused on their presentations. She had perfected that shell, eyebrows a bit raised, eyes focused. But her thoughts were on Daniel. What would it be like for them to meet again? Would he recognize her? Would he see her as a success, a noticeable success? Obviously, he was. She would check his credentials when the lights came up. She, well, not too much of a failure. After all, here she was, a delegate from Hopkins, at this conference, by invitation only. So, no, not too much of a failure.

She watched as the panel acknowledged the applause. The delegates filed from the room; the panelists exited by a side door. She thought about running after them. No, she decided, too high school, much too high school. And with a thousand attendees spread throughout the convention centers, would she even find him? If it is meant to be, she thought, it will happen. Then she sat to figure out how to make it so.

John stood in the back of the room, watching, waiting for her to leave. He approached her as she turned into the aisle.

"Are you sitting with anyone at lunch?"

Claire smiled and said nothing.

"Let's have a quick drink before we go in. I'm at the speakers' table. I'm sure they could manage one more space."

Claire's smile brightened. "That would be delightful."

John placed his hand lightly on her shoulder as they maneuvered through the crowd.

By the next day, life had changed. "So much to catch up on," Daniel smiled at Claire.

Claire toyed with the cocktail napkin, folded it in half, in quarters, in eights, noticed the hangnail on her middle finger, resisted the impulse to bite it, to put her hand in her mouth. She placed her right hand under the table, picked at the cuticle on her thumb, felt the stab of pain, then placed the napkin, unfolded this time, against it to stop the bleeding.

She tilted her head to the right. Daniel remembered that. She's nervous, he thought.

"Well, here you are, a big shot. On the panel with all the big shots." Claire winced. She wanted to sound – what? educated? sophisticated? worldly? Instead she realized that she sounded exactly as she felt – an impostor in this world of learned experts. A poseur.

Daniel reached under the table for her hand. She still picked at her thumbs, he noticed, wondering just how he had remembered that. She hasn't changed that much, he thought.

Claire started at the touch, somehow still familiar. Daniel too was surprised at how easily the movement came. He smiled. "I guess some things we remember." He patted her hand, released it. "I didn't mean to be forward."

Claire laughed. "Well, I surely didn't expect to come here and feel like a teenager again. An impostor, maybe, but not a lovesick teenager." There, she thought, I've done it, spoken my biggest fears. Said it out loud. She laughed, hoping he would see her words as a joke. So he'll know how grown-up I am, how secure. She blushed. An act. I'm even thinking like a child. An act. She took a deep breath.

Daniel leaned back. "You are anything but an impostor, Claire. And anything but a teenager." He paused. "After all this time."

He cleared his throat. "So, tell me about you, about your life, about these fifteen years. Are you married? And what are you doing at this stuffy conference of old men?" He looked at her left hand. No ring.

Claire lifted her chin, placed her folded hands on the table. "Well, I'm at Hopkins, the School of Public Health. I started as a research assistant, or really the assistant to the assistant, and after ten years plus have ascended to my current lofty position. I'm assistant to the assistant director of one of the branches. Mostly administrative work, rewriting, translating scientific mumbo-jumbo into readable articles for publication, for non-scientific journals, the press, keeping the Hopkins name in the fore. You know, sort of PR for the masses, or at least the masses who have pockets deep enough to fund us. I got my MPH there, mostly night classes now. A slow, slogging process, I'm afraid, but I'm glad I stuck it out to see the light at the end of the tunnel, or at least to enter another tunnel."

Daniel lifted his glass in a toast. "Well, here's to you. My successful Claire."

A silence followed, uncomfortable for both of them. Claire broke the silence. "You know, I'm not exactly your Claire, am I?"

She allowed Daniel to stew in his own discomfort, then laughed. "It's a joke, Daniel. I'm really not seventeen any longer. Much water under the bridge since then. And I understand, all of it. I do, really. You absolutely did the right thing, for both of us. I know that. No need to, well, you know."

She inhaled, sat more erect in her chair. "And so now, tell me the Book of Daniel."

Once, in a cocktail lounge in Boston, after a second Stinger, he called her Clairedelune.

Claire became alert; the fog of the scotch evaporated. "Why did you call me that?" Her mind was woolly.

"I remember your mother calling you that. How it always made you smile."

Claire left her throat clench. "Yes." She focused on the cocktail glass before her, swirled it on its slim stem. "My mother, my father, my niece. No one else." She didn't raise her eyes.

"Not even I?" Daniel leaned his head to the left.

She lifted her head, looked at the ceiling." Well, maybe even you," she responded. "But only on special occasions."

Daniel reached for her hand." But any time I'm with you is a special occasion."

Claire nodded, swallowed. She had expected that response. She looked in his eyes. "Would that some could be ordinary."

She wanted to take those words back as soon as she heard herself speak. But words cannot be unsaid. She forced a smile. "I don't know where that came from. It's fine that our occasions are. Fantasy is always better, no?"

Daniel reached for his drink and emptied the glass. "Let's see if we can see the swans." And they rose and walked into a Beacon Street twilight.

They met, exciting, she thought, in cities from the Atlantic to the Pacific, once in Tokyo. Once a year, not always the same conference. One time she was a speaker, though in a minor session, Daniel in the audience cheering her on. Nice, she thought, her secret lover out there.

And, in the way of all lovers, they were sure no one suspected. And, in the way of all lovers, everyone knew. Everyone who worked with him, or her, everyone who was included in those conference dinners the two arranged, large enough so that they could be anonymous, they thought. The two emitted a sexual energy that all but the most obtuse could not fail to recognize. They perceived no disapproval. Free-wheeling sexual hook-ups had been standard operating procedure at these conferences long before their liaison.

But they thought the secret was theirs, and it added to the glamour, the intensity of their encounters.

Daniel was the first to say I love you, and Claire believed him. She kept silent, for she knew it was the kind of love that was present only during sex, and their phone calls, infrequent, always starting with a question about the World Health Organization or African mortality statistics, and once, on tuberculosis rates in Baltimore City. It was Daniel who called, always, and they dispensed with business forthwith, content with the extended silences that followed "How are you?"

They laughed quietly as they discussed conferences, plotting to stay at the same hotel. Once they flew on the same plane, though they didn't sit together.

Yes, Claire knew, Daniel loved her. But through a filter – of youth, of clandestine couplings, where all was light and sun-filled and replete with underwear of silk and lace. She had no illusions and that was fine with her, though she did allow herself fantasies, at night, as she drifted off to sleep. Daniel was the only love she allowed there. Only Daniel. And sometimes Viktor.

We say everyone knew, leaving out a minor player. The wife, who somehow felt sad every time Daniel caught a cab for O'Hare, who was jittery on the days he was away, even during his check-ins to see how she was, and not-quite-trusting of his vigorous amorous advances upon his return. She said nothing. What, she thought, was to be gained?

And Daniel, he was a decent sort. He loved the wife. He loved Claire. But Claire had a life, a good one, glamourous it could be said. And the wife, well, she had Daniel.

Thirty-eight

She snapped the clasp on her Lady Baltimore luggage; it felt good to throw in underwear, sweaters, blouses without worrying about wrinkles. She took care, though, with the two suits she had packed – one grey lightweight wool that buttoned on the side, the other a heavier-weight rich chocolate brown with mink trim around the collar. High-heeled pumps, brown suede, were secure in their sock casings, and she made sure to wrap the crocodile skin bag in a slip, protected. Better off than its original owner, she thought, though both might appear a bit dated for these times.

These clothes, this packing, always a silk nightgown, just in case. And just-in-case usually happened. An old friend, sometimes someone new, but, with one long-ago exception, always pleasurable, pleasant, sometimes exciting. Claire folded the nightgown carefully and placed it between the suits. She smiled as she thought, last one, last time. Lesson learned. Always stop while you're ahead. No more, not even with old friends. She paused, well, perhaps only with old friends.

For that night at dinner they had learned of Sam's fate, Sam, one of the ones who didn't give her too hard a time. She remembered how they had laughed at breakfast when his place remained empty. The table the group had commandeered that first morning had, indeed, become their table.

The unwritten rule of every conference she had ever attended: you show up for meals, for meetings, no matter how hung over, no matter how enamored. With few exceptions, those who were of no consequence and who didn't matter anyway, the contingent laughed, drank, ate together and cast an approving, if blind, eye, to any assignations, as long of course, as they didn't involve any of those feelings that some insisted on attaching to such liaisons. With few exceptions, it worked well, and those who got hurt, well, they just left the team. Still respected, academically, professionally, but an element of camaraderie was withheld. As one might imagine, this rarely affected the male members of the group.

165

There were a few sniggers when Sam's chair remained empty at the 7:30 breakfast. When they realized that no one had seen him at any of the morning sessions, and he was nowhere to be found at lunchtime, eyebrows were definitely raised. Not cricket, their eyes said. Out of bounds.

By late afternoon, the word had spread. Apparent heart attack. Found in his bed, alone.

That evening, the group gathered for the awards dinner, two of them honorees, the moderator made the announcement. A moment of silence. Claire stood, head bowed, picturing the last time she had seen him. All those white teeth, the two front ones slightly overlapped, like the fiancé, she realized. Always gave him a bit of a boyish look that she found appealing. He had been a good friend, and a supporter of her career.

She felt a movement at her right as her tablemate rose to speak. "A good man, a conscientious scholar, a rigorous researcher. Let us raise a glass to his memory."

The voice from the podium: "Well said. Let us remember him and celebrate his life." And the dinner had continued as planned.

That night, in her hotel room, alone, Claire decided. A chapter ended, an enjoyable one. But over. She reached for the miniature of bourbon she had been served on the plane, poured it into her tooth glass, and toasted Sam, and herself. The end of an era, she thought. The end of so much. Tomorrow, a new start.

The next day, striding through the airport with no time to waste, Claire felt her left leg give way. She fell, face forward, onto the marble floor. People gathered; a stranger helped her up; a second presented a handkerchief to wipe the blood from her face; a woman appeared with a wet paper towel.

"More embarrassed than hurt," she managed to say, mumbling her thanks, grateful that she was among strangers.

Thirty-nine

Claire stood at Hutzler's Gift Wrap Department, waited her turn, slipped her left foot from her shoe, wiggled her toes to ease the pain. Patience, she exhaled and turned her thoughts to what she would cook for her dinner. No, she decided, it'll be take-out from the Blue Jay. Greek salad, pound cake for dessert, or maybe baklava. A reward for having just the salad, and for stopping downtown to buy this gift.

Finally her turn, the wrapper took her purchases, two onesies, one yellow, one white. She pointed to the foil paper featuring diapers, diaper pins, teething rings, and pulled the sheet from the drawer when Claire nodded.

"Baby shower, right?" She folded the ends into sharp corners and taped them. "Ribbon color?" Claire felt, and heard, her stomach rumble, rested her elbow on the counter. "Oh, you choose. Anything is fine."

Ribbons, bows, she thought. They use them for something she couldn't quite place, the scores of showers attended running together in her memory. No, that's wedding showers. They use the ribbons for a bouquet. Yes. She smiled that she remembered it, the rehearsal bouquet.

Another Saturday afternoon, another shower, this time for a woman from her book group, this pregnancy longed for and long in coming. Claire was delighted for her. It wasn't the babies she minded. It was the interminable showers, always the same, each following a pattern which everyone except Claire seemed to find intriguing. Or maybe others, a few, could smile just as disingenuously as she.

The following day, Claire was the third to arrive, and by mid-afternoon, all were going along with the fantasy that the mother-to-be would be surprised, which, when she arrived at ten minutes after the appointed hour, she managed to convey in an almost-credible way.

167

Gifts opened, packages of diapers stacked, towels, receiving blankets, a coming-home-from-the-hospital gown embroidered, white-on-white, each gift dutifully listed and described with the giver's name beside it, the next order of business was the games. Claire glanced to the dining room to see if a bar was set up. A punch bowl, only a punch bowl, no bar. She smiled and glanced around the room, sneaking a look at her watch. No leaving until the cake, which she had also seen sitting beside the now-empty punch bowl, was cut and served, all requiring the obligatory oohs and aahs about the thick white frosting and *baby-to-be* spelled out in green, or yellow.

Give me strength, she muttered to herself, and leaned back in her chair.

The needle and thread had been brought out and Trish, the guest of honor had her hand over her eyes as she held out her right wrist. The hostess lowered the thread up and down three times. "Now take your wrist away, slowly." The group had their eyes on the needle at the end of the thread. Slowly it moved back and forth.

"A boy," someone called out. Claire reached over and hugged the mother-to-be, who, eyes lowered, said in a low voice, "We just want it to be healthy." Claire leaned in. "It will be. I feel it in my bones." The two returned their attention to the party, the hostess going to each who proffered their wrists.

"Now you, Claire. You never know."

Claire, not sure who had spoken, felt that she had no choice but to comply, so important was it to be perceived as a good sport, pushed her gold bracelet higher on her arm, and closed her eyes.

"Okay, just take your wrist away." Claire complied and watched the needle. It did not move. All were silent. Until, from across the room, an angel-savior called out. "Such silliness. Mine never moved when I did it and Octavia arrived almost without warning. And she's enough for eight, believe me. We were prescient when we named her."

The group burst into relieved laughter, louder and with a bit more hysteria than they had anticipated.

The hostess, who by this time had stashed the needle and thread in a drawer of the side table resolving never to do that ritual again, stood, clapped her hands, and called out, "Who wants cake?" Amid chatter that was a bit too buoyant to bear any resemblance to truth, the group moved to the dining room.

Thirty minutes later, Claire made her farewells, and headed to the door. The woman who had saved the day made her way to her. "I'm Harriet and I hate these things." She smiled and the two walked to Claire's car. "Really, don't you hate these things? Way too much estrogen in one room. I.Q. drops for every ounce of butter cream frosting."

Claire heard her a sound come from her throat, hysteria combined with a burst of tears and laughter. She fished in her purse for her keys. "You are absolutely the best. Would you like a ride? Or how about stopping by my house first? Have a bit of libation."

"Always, I thought you'd never ask. I'll follow in my car. Where do you live, anyway?"

And so, after an introduction of slightly-stale crackers and cheese, bourbon for Claire, scotch for Harriet, a friendship began. For Claire, it filled a void left by Naomi's departure, although it would never be the same for her, without Naomi. For Harriet, Claire was different, a breath of fresh air, away from the staid, hide-bound toddler mothers and dutiful wives of her boring Northwood neighborhood. Every house the same, every family in it stamped from the same mold, at least in the appearance they presented to the world, for appearance was of the essence, if not the essence. Harriet felt that she could say anything to Claire, and she did.

"Sanctimonious twits," she said to Claire, and then laughed. "Hmm, perhaps that's why I'm no longer invited to coffee in the mornings. And, you know, it kind of makes me proud not to fit in." She hesitated. "But then I've never really fit in, I don't think." She shrugged her shoulders. "*C'est la vie*, as they say on the continent."

They got together every few weeks, a Saturday lunch, a visit at Claire's apartment, once, dinner with Harriet's family, though they both realized that they would not do that again. The kids seemed enchanted, saw Claire like an exotic maiden aunt. The husband viewed her as a threat, someone to stoke Harriet's dangerous fires of independence and unconventionality. Claire recognized this, though she kept her thoughts to herself.

One Saturday afternoon, Harriet got to meet Fritz, and drove home picturing his good looks and suave manner. Dangerous notions. She smiled at forbidden whimseys. Months later she was introduced to Viktor and believed him dour and strait-laced, though she realized that there must be some loose strings for the married Czech to be with this woman he obviously loved. Ah, she thought, more freedom to be jealous of.

And it was she whom Claire would count on, later, when it mattered.

Forty

The funeral was scheduled for 11:00 a.m., Sts. Phillip and James Church. Though Fritz was never a church goer, Claire thought that this was the best way. A formal goodbye, complete with music, priest and Latin. No mass, though; she had enough of Fritz in her to know where and when to draw a line. A simple service. He would be buried beside Lily, in Druid Ridge Cemetery, a stone's throw from the notorious *Black Aggie*. Claire imagined him smiling as the fraternities performing their initiation rites and fueled by bottles of National Boh, dared one another to sit in the lap of that draped, melancholy and mysterious marble woman seated at the Agnus family plot in the south-facing side of the cemetery in Pikesville. Word was that her stony eyes turned red at night. Sit on her lap at midnight and you would meet your own end within two weeks. Teens, often fueled by beer and bravado, travelled to Druid Ridge at night to test the rumor. It was terrifying, exhilarating and the stuff of Baltimore urban legends for years. Oh, yes, Claire thought, Fritz would comfort Lily, who was most likely perpetually miffed at the empty beer bottles that the visitors left in their stead.

Claire forced herself to think of that, to smile, not dwell on Fritz's death, her own loneliness, the realization that, really, she had no family now. She was, and would remain, alone.

Her colleagues had shown sympathy. Those who had met Fritz over the years remembered him as charming, handsome, one who made them feel important without trying. Someone they could be themselves with, without artifice. She had invited only one to the funeral. Viktor. Always Viktor.

She was the one the hospital had contacted. Louisa would never forgive her for that. Claire had called Charles with the news, to make sure that Louisa was not alone when she learned of the accident. Stepping on to North Avenue after a lunch at Nate's and Leon's, turning his head to say a laughing goodbye, Fritz had stepped directly into the path of an oncoming car. No one's fault, Claire told herself. Just an ending. And she was glad that he had been laughing, had been happy, had been with friends, at the end. Charles phoned Claire later that evening; Louisa had taken the news badly, as they feared she would. He had called her doctor and she was resting. They would take it one day at a time. Charles felt it would be best if Louisa made the arrangements for Fritz. Claire demurred. She would take the lead on this, this last time.

Louisa did not contact Claire; Charles said that they would attend, that Louisa wanted to be in the first row of the church and did not want to see Claire.

Fair enough, thought Claire, who knew that the cavernous church would be filled, that she could be easily lost in the crowd. She didn't need to be seen or ride in a limousine. To be there was enough.

There were empty chairs on both sides of Louisa and Charles at the gravesite. Claire wondered where Charlotte was; she would ask Charles later. She stood, Viktor at her side, in the midst of the mourners. The priest said some words. Claire did not hear them; she was watching Louisa sob, Charles holding her hand, his arm around her shoulders. Viktor glanced over at Claire, took her gloved hand in his, gently, subtly. There was no one there to see. Claire thought about Naomi, wished she were there, closed her eyes. Oh, Naomi, why did you leave? Where did you go? Claire would visit with her that night, imagine Naomi sitting with her. They would cry together. Naomi would understand it all.

She squeezed Viktor's hand. And for now, she had Viktor. Fritz had known the first time he had seen them together. He predicted this, exactly. She felt a movement beside her. Viktor extricated his hand from hers, fumbled in his pocket for his handkerchief. Claire glanced over. Viktor, stoic Viktor, who seldom laughed, who smiled easily only when they were in bed together, had tears running down his face, falling, dripping onto the collar of his overcoat. His eyes were closed. She didn't know

172

if he knew what she had seen. She said nothing, and felt the instant attack of a migraine.

The crowd dispersed, shaking Louisa's hand, Charles's hand; those who knew Claire murmured their condolences. There was no gathering after the burial; each went his own way, quiet with his own thoughts. Charles passed close enough to touch, Louisa on his far side. Neither made eye contact. Claire was relieved.

Viktor led Claire back to his car. They waited as the crowd dispersed. He made no move to start the engine. He stared straight ahead. Without turning to face Claire, he said, "You know, that is the first time I can remember crying. I'm sure I cried as a child, but certainly not often. I didn't cry when I realized that my mother wasn't coming back; I didn't cry when I stepped out of my house and knew that there was no place to go, no one to go to. I don't cry when I think about the war, about those I will never see again. But for Fritz, I cry. He was one-in-a-million, as you people say. I will never forget him. He made me feel..." Viktor stopped, swallowed, tilted his head. He reached for the ignition. "I'm sure you're exhausted. Let's go home."

Claire closed her eyes. Viktor had called her apartment "home." Sobs shook her body. She couldn't tell if it was because of Fritz or because of Viktor's words.

Viktor used Claire's keys to open the door, took her in his arms when they stepped inside.

"Stay. Will you stay?" Claire murmured.

"Of course."

Later that evening, looking down at the plate of scrambled eggs she had assembled for their dinner, Claire whispered, "Don't you need to call? To say that you won't be home?"

Viktor reached for her hand. "No. I am not expected this night."

Fritz had left a will; his attorney was the executor. Claire thought this a wise move on Fritz's part. One less dramatic scenario. By the time she received the letter outlining its terms, Louisa had already been to his apartment, taken all that she wanted or thought valuable. In a trashcan, Claire found his silver lighter, something to remember him by. There was nothing else worth fighting over, she decided, though she packed up a few books that she remembered from Sylvan Cliffs. The past is the past, another country. She had read that somewhere, sometime, but could not remember when. True, she thought. Just another lesson from literature. Those seem to imprint themselves a bit deeper than those lessons one gets from life.

She imagined Louisa's reaction to Fritz's meager estate; for Louisa, there was never enough. Claire wasn't surprised; she concluded that both Fritz and Lily lived the good life on only an adequate income. That fit, she thought. Well, good for them. Good for them.

Forty-one

Claire,

How dare you try to contact my daughter. You are dead to us, dead to my family. I will put my legal team on you if you try this again. Harassment. Pure harassment.

You have done enough. Leave us alone.

You are evil. You are a torturer. And God will punish you. And when that happens, I hope I am there to see it. I will laugh and applaud.

You are worthless. You have always been worthless. And everyone knows it. You fool no one.

Leave us alone. Or else.

Dear Claire,

Please don't try to contact me again. I'm sorry, really, I am.

It's just – well, all this craziness in this family. Mother – well, you know. I'm staying away as much as I can. Whenever I see her, she talks about you, about Lilygram. She's so angry. I guess I don't have to tell you.

If she knew we were in contact, she'd blow a gasket – or another gasket. She asks every time I see her. And, honestly, I'm just not up to lying. I can only stand so much, and I don't want to add to the horror of any time I see her, which is hardly ever. That is why I didn't come to Faht's funeral. For now, the only way I can save myself is to be free of all of you, away from all this crazy drama.

I am sorry, Clairedelune. I know this is painful
– and my heart aches too. But sometimes you
must make difficult decisions to save yourself.
This should be a book, except no one would
believe it.

I will never forget you. You were always my
shining star. I wish it could be different. Maybe
one day. But not now.

Please don't try to get in touch. Don't.

Charlotte

I'm not doing so well in the letter department, Claire thought.
No more Lily, no more Fritz. Maybe it's time to just let this one
be. Maybe I'm just done.

A few weeks later the city was in flames. At least that's how
the newscasters put it, and, from what Claire saw on television,
they were pretty much right. D'Alessandro had called in the
National Guard; she could see them stationed at her corner. The
line of shops across St. Paul Street were closed, though there had
been no disturbances that she knew of. McInally had called her
on Sunday evening; the School facilities were closed, at least for
the first part of the week. Victor had been with her when the call
came. Gay Street, Broadway was shut down.

Viktor turned to her. "Stay or go? Maybe you'd like me here,
to stay with you?"

"You need to be home; you need to figure out how you're
going to get home; I think Orleans Street is closed. And call me
when you get there. That I do ask. I'll be fine here. I'm not afraid.
Oscar is my protection; he is like a lion."

And Claire was grateful that Viktor's departure was a reluctant
one.

The next morning, Oscar wound his way around Claire's ankles as she opened the can of 9Lives. As she turned to place the bowl on the floor, her right leg buckled. She reached to steady herself with her left hand; the bowl clattered to the floor. She turned to look, then landed, hard, on the kitchen floor. Oscar left his perch on the chair and came to investigate, licking the tuna medley from Claire's robe.

She sat, her back against the refrigerator, and stroked the cat's fur. "Oh, Oscar. This is not good, not good at all."

Part Four

Forty-two

Claire had done her research, anticipated and prepared herself for the outcome. Still, a professional opinion. A second? A third? She followed the exacting procedure, what she would have advised another to do. Leave nothing to chance, to a misinterpretation, a subjective misreading. Though it won't be, she thought. And it wasn't.

The neurological exam, the EMG complete with the pinprick barrage, the serious demeanor of the physicians, both of them, to deliver the news she already knew.

Well, at least Faht is dead, she thought. I won't have to tell him. She then considered just whom she would tell. Not many, and not yet. She had requested two days off, some personal business, she said. Now she regretted it. Too many days to fill, to think, to plan. And whom to tell. And when. Viktor, like Claire, already knew.

She pulled into the garage space, entered her building through the back door. Walking to the mailbox lobby, she extricated letters and two catalogues that had been stuffed tightly into the space. She riffled through them as she waited for the elevator. Let me think of other things, she thought. A night TV perhaps. *Bewitched.* Perhaps Samantha can twitch her nose and I'll be my old self again. Which I need to be. By Monday morning. Mind over matter, she thought. Surely there is a German word that would describe it better. She would ask Viktor.

And then she saw it, the letter.

Claire recognized the handwriting. Naomi. A letter from Naomi, arriving this day. What is it about me and letters, she thought. They never bode well. And today, arriving today. Wouldn't you just know it.

She held Naomi's letter between the fingers of her right hand, and as she waited for the elevator door to slide open and her heart to stop pounding, glanced through the other pieces in the mailbox. Bills, advertisements, an invitation with a calligraphy address. I'll handle this like an adult, she told herself, handle all of this like an adult. I'll change clothes, fix a drink, settle down on the couch and then open her letter. Then I'll think about today, consider my tomorrows.

But she had torn open the envelop before she reached her door. She didn't change her clothes; she didn't fix a drink; she shrugged off her coat and settled on the sofa. Oh, Naomi, she thought, as she pulled the lined sheets from the envelop, at least this gets my mind off myself.

> *Dear Claire,*
>
> *I'm writing to you at your old address – and, if I know you –you are still there – at least that is what I'm hoping.*
>
> *It's been years – and I am sorry – you are still a part of me – I have conversations with you, and you always tell me the right thing to do – though I don't always do it.*
>
> *So here is what I've done – part of it you would approve of, so I'll start with that –*
>
> *I am married. Can you believe it? He is a good-enough man and he offers me a life I think I'm ready for – steady, safe, boring. I know, I know, don't lecture me, not even in your head.*

Claire moved to the dining room table, pushed her papers aside, cleared a space. This will take a while, she thought. She pulled a cigarette from her purse, lit it with the Fritz's lighter, and continued reading.

> *His name is Charlie Speer, and he sells suspenders. I know. Please don't laugh – or laugh with me, not at me. He travels most weeks – so I*

179

will have lots of time for myself, and for that I am grateful. And Charlie has saved me from a hard life. I know that. And for that I am grateful as well. I consider it a fair deal. I make him happy, Claire. He says that I make him laugh. And he likes my cooking. I cook now. Can you believe that?

So that is the part I think you approve of. Plus I told him that I know you, told him all about you. He is impressed.

He has a trip planned to Baltimore next month and asked if I wanted to go along, to see you. And so I thought that was a sign that I write. I wanted to wait until I was on my feet. And now I am – also on my back – a lot – on weekends only. So you don't have to worry there.

You can see from the return address that we live in Harrisburg, not so far away.

But before you answer, I want to tell you the part that you would not approve of. And before you read it, let me just say, I know, I know. It is stupid, it does not bode well, to use your words. I knew all that and did it anyway. But I think one day I'll make it right – just not now, not any time soon.

So – to Charlie, my name is Janet. I changed it when I left Baltimore – you know, a new name, a new life. Charlie doesn't know about Naomi, or the shop or the jobs before. He just thinks I'm a hick from Hagerstown (which I am), who worked in a department store in Baltimore (Gutman's) and then decided to move to Pennsylvania where we met while I worked at the front desk at the motel where he stayed. We struck it off. He is a good man. Not real smart, but not stupid either. Just naive. So he believes what he wants to believe and I let him. You might call that kindness, not deception.

Oh, I haven't ever written a letter like this. In fact this is the first letter I've written since that one to you – and that was a long time ago.

Now, I understand if you want to tear this letter into 1,000 pieces. But I hope you won't. Not to be presumptuous (now that is another Claire word), but I think I will hear from you.

So try not to think of me as dishonest. Can you call me "creative"?

Also, I don't think I'm as smart as I was – book-smart, I mean. I miss your influence. Also, Naomi says hello and that she misses you. I will watch my mailbox every day.

Love,

Janet Speer (AKA Naomi)

Forty-three

Six weeks and three doctors' appointments later, though no new information was garnered by these encounters, Claire felt something of the old Naomi there as she hugged her goodbye, the first, the only, time during their visit. She left her hand on the doorknob after she closed the door, not able, or wanting, to move.

Where have you gone, Joe DiMaggio? The words of Simon and Garfunkel were all she could hear. *Where have you gone, Joe DiMaggio? Our nation turns its lonely eyes to you.*

Claire pressed her forehead to the door, weeping with sobs so deep that her stomach hurt. The first time she had cried, the first time since she knew what lay ahead. Where have you gone, Naomi? What happened to you? Where have you gone?

For Claire knew that her Naomi was gone, a trade-in, she supposed, for security, a life where she thought she didn't have to be worried, afraid. Claire swallowed and walked to the sofa, sat, hands folded in her lap. "I understand." She whispered these words aloud. "I understand. But I miss you. When we met, you were free, happy, trusting the universe to provide." Except, Claire thought, I see now that the universe doesn't provide, and it looks like we all pay the price for being who we are. She walked to the bedroom, found a handkerchief, blew her nose. I loved those times, loved you, she thought, sitting down on the bed. And now, now you are just ordinary. My loss, the world's loss. Everything is a loss.

Claire took a deep breath. I hope that you are at least somewhat happy. But your spark, your brio (she smiled as she imagined the old Naomi's reaction if she had used that word), is dead. Do you miss it? Do you miss Naomi? She was sorry that she hadn't had the courage to ask.

"You were my outrageous friend, the one who gave me courage, inspired me to stand up for myself, who pushed me to be more than I thought I could be." Claire heard her words, and was glad that she lived alone, could say anything she wanted out loud. "I wanted us to be like we used to be, wanted us to be who we used to be. I wanted you to see who I have become; I wanted to tell you how responsible you are for so much of that.

"And now life has changed so much for both of us, I wonder if our memories are ever the truth."

Claire kicked off her shoes, returned to the living room, closed her eyes. I guess I was the one you looked to today, she thought, to see how it is to be normal. Boring it is, Naomi, and not even safe, definitely not safe. It is never safe. I think you know that, deep down. And you'll be fine; you just won't be Naomi. And I'll be fine; I just will no longer be Claire.

She had wanted to tell Naomi what was happening, what was wrong, what she had decided to do. Claire wanted her to hear, to understand, wanted Naomi to approve, to tell her that she was right, that she was doing the right thing. But the part of Naomi that Claire needed to reach, that wasn't there. She closed her eyes and spoke again "What did you do with that part of yourself? Did you push it down? Did you destroy it? Just to be safe?" And, she thought, how different is what you've done from the path I've chosen? I wish we could have talked, really talked, like in the old days.

Claire bent down to pick up the bowl of chips, ate one, then another, without tasting them, and walked to the window. She saw Naomi, waiting on the corner of St. Paul and 31st Streets. She tapped on the window, pressed her fingers to her lips. Naomi didn't look up. Claire saw her wave to the green Dodge Dart as it rolled to a stop. The driver leaned over to open the passenger-side door. She got in.

Claire turned away, lit a cigarette, refreshed her glass with one-finger of bourbon, and sat, remembering.

*

Forty-four

Claire parked in the lot on Mulberry Street and headed the one block south to Howard, to meet Harriet. It had been months since they had seen one another. The walk took longer than usual. Everything took longer than usual, she thought, and when she arrived at the Virginia Dare Restaurant, she saw that Harriet had a table for them. Shit, she thought, as she maneuvered between the tables to her seat. She had wanted to arrive first, be seated when Harriet appeared.

Harriet caught sight of her as she passed the display cases of pastries and chocolates, and sat straighter in her chair. As soon as Claire got to the table, she said, "And what is this? Why didn't you tell me? What's happened? A fall? What?"

Claire was grateful for the barrage of questions, and sat down more gracefully than she had managed in a while. "Well, which do you want first? Or should we just order and then relax and talk? I vote for the latter." Claire picked up the menu and studied it, wondering how many more restaurant meals there would be for her. All these little details, parts of living that you take for granted. No more. Nothing for granted these days.

She signaled to the waitress, potato soup, quiche Lorraine. Sandwiches and salads were already proving difficult to eat. Shit, she thought, just shit. Harriet gave her order, but did not take her eyes from her friend across the table. "I'll have the same."

Harriet continued, "Okay, that is that. Now, what is going on? You're making me nervous. A cane? What is that for? What is going on?"

"Well, it's not good." Claire put her hands in her lap, told Harriet the story, her news. "I think I've had symptoms for a while now, a year at least, maybe longer. I just thought I was getting clumsy. But I'm getting worse, obviously. Thus, the cane. I can't trust my pins to keep me upright all the time. At first, I thought it might be polio, a late case, post vaccine. Wouldn't that be irony?"

Harriet mirrored Claire's stoicism as she heard the diagnosis. "I don't know what to say." The two were quiet as their meal was

184

served. Finally, only the quiche crusts left on their plates, Harriet said, "What can I do? How can I help? Just ask. You know I'll be there, here, whatever, whenever, wherever."

Claire nodded. "I know. And there is something. Will you take Oscar?"

But Harriet did more than that, and Claire marveled that her friend possessed as much organization and know-how as she herself did. And it felt remarkable, and unfamiliar, to be taken care of. It was Harriet who drove Claire for yet another EMG, all those needles, the results confirming what the previous tests said.

When work became impracticable, Claire left with little fuss, as she had wanted. She told no one the details, yet they all knew. She waited until she was back in her apartment to read the notes that the staff had written. She allowed herself to cry, the second time since the initial diagnosis. It was Harriet who researched social security disability payments, who encouraged Claire to apply, though Claire knew it was unnecessary, pointless. It was Harriet who visited twice a week, proudly bringing eclairs and Napoleons from Nate's and Leon's on North Avenue. She never knew its connection to Fritz's death, and Claire never told her. Still, it was Fritz she thought of when Harriet displayed them on the Dresden china that had been in the Mueller family for generations.

It was Harriet who asked about her life, not Viktor. He already knew. Viktor knew all there was to know about Claire. At least he thought he did.

During one visit Harriet asked Claire about her work, how she had become "such an exalted figure." Claire laughed, shook her head.

"You know, it just happened. I would have liked to have been able to tell you that I had a plan, a strategy. That I knew, that I wanted to have this, this profession. I guess you'd call it. But it seems to have just happened. I did the only thing I knew how to do, work hard, I guess, do my best. And then take advantage of

185

opportunities as they presented themselves. So much of it was luck, really."

She told Harriet about her abrupt transfer from the City Health Department to the Hopkins campus. "I always thought that my sister had something to do with it. Not that she ever expected it to turn out the way it did. I think she thought that I would be fired. And why I wasn't, well, who can figure that out? Just a quirk of fate. And I think that's what my career has been, just one quirk of fate after another.

"Now they talk about the 'women's movement.' Betty Friedan, Gloria Steinem, that Abzug woman with the hats. And I like that. I like that a lot. And it is only you that I'd tell how little I was a part of that. I just came to work every day and did my job. I must have had something like that in my mind during my 'fiancé debacle,' but it never seemed to be out of principle or ambition. The closest I came was when something came over me and I went out and bought a red leather briefcase from Tuerke's, with my initials embossed in gold lettering. I liked my job, I guess, and then, almost without my thinking, it became a career. But it was never a driving force for me. Would that it had been. I would have felt prouder, more fulfilled, I think.

Harriet leaned back in her seat. "I think you don't give yourself enough credit. Surely you could have taken the easy way out, married, like the rest of us, given all this up for," she hesitated, "for a boring life like the rest of us."

Claire laughed. "You ascribe too much glamor to going to work every day, Harriet. There's a price we pay for whatever decisions we make, or are made for us. You're just honest enough to see your life without having to make it into something more, or less.

"That's why we're friends, I guess. Honesty doesn't play well to the ladies-who-lunch crowd."

Harriet brought over two glasses, poured a finger of bourbon into both. "And Viktor? Why Viktor?"

186

Claire looked into her glass. "You know, the first time my father met Viktor, and they liked one another right away, he warned me about him. I guess you'd say it was a warning. He said that he was 'broken.' That was the word he used. Viktor's past, his experiences before he came to this country. Faht said that they could never be erased.

"And he was right. Our experiences can't be erased. And they break us. Eventually they break us. And I think Viktor and I are both broken somehow, in ways that fit together. Not like normal couples. But we understand one another, in our own way, I think. There have been other men, you know that. But it is Viktor. Yes. Only Viktor."

"Regrets?" Harriet asked, and realized that it was she who wanted to confide her own. "Children?"

Claire smiled, massaged her left arm and elbow, worked it gently to try to straighten it out. "Oh, you know. I remember Lily, my mother Lily, saying once 'what never makes you laugh never makes you cry.' I thought at the time it was an odd thing for a mother to tell her child." Claire shook her head. "Ah, these odd memories that come back, unbidden. And don't they tell a story, without words, to be sure. But I don't know. I don't think I'm a child person. It never seemed relevant, to be honest."

"You know, I think that this motherhood thing, well, we just are never really truthful about it. I will tell you, only you, that two of my children are like strange aliens to me. Oh, I love them, I guess, but I really don't like them not at all. I would never choose to spend any time with them at all unless I had to. But Octavia, who was such a trial at the beginning, she's the one, she really does bring me joy. Without trying. And the others ignore her, on purpose, I think. They know how to hurt. They're bullies, I think. One day they'll turn on each other, you can bet on that. And meantime, I'm just the one who has dinner on the table." Harriet's words startled her, verbalizing these feelings that somehow had to be said. She shook her head.

"So sorry, this is not supposed to be about me. It's just that I feel that I can say anything to you."

187

"Every choice we make, or choose to go along with, has a price, don't you think?

Harriet remained silent, thankful for her friend's candor, honesty, though she thought that the price Claire was paying was too high.

Forty-five

The third time Claire cried was when she handed Oscar and his canned food over to Harriet.

"Are you sure? I can come by every couple of days and feed him, you know. You can leave food out for cats that way. You don't have to give him up. Really, you don't."

But Claire knew that she did. Part of saying goodbye, piece by piece. Her job, her cat. She could no longer straighten either arm. And now her goodbye to Harriet. A funeral before the funeral, she thought, as she dressed for her friend's visit. Viktor, who was now there every evening, stayed through the morning, had left a tray set for them – the teapot, the cakes from Eddie's covered with waxed paper. All Claire had to do was plug in the kettle. He left the door off the latch, for Harriet's visit.

Harriet knew when she saw her. This would be her last visit. And what was there left to say?

But it was Claire who wanted to talk, to say a proper goodbye, to explain, though she knew that Harriet needed no explanation.

"This is not a time for tears, except for saying goodbye to Oscar. You know that I've thought about this, considered it. And I want to leave this way, loving my life, the people in it, not struggling for breath, a burden, so that people are relieved when it's over. And it would be over soon, anyway, so what is a few months?"

"You don't have to do this, you know. I'm here; Viktor's here."

Claire shifted in her chair, reached town to massage her right ankle. She wore her black Papagallo flats.

"To cease upon that midnight with no pain."

Seeing Harriet's look, Claire said, "Keats. I wish I had discovered poetry earlier. It was Viktor, you know, who introduced me. Not any academic institution. He's been my real education. What he knows, who he is. I wonder, sometimes, who he would have been, could have been, without the war. But for

189

me, I am lucky to have had him in my life. Faht, Viktor – how many women have had as much?"

Harriet swallowed hard to keep the tears at bay, stood to come closer. Claire stopped her. "Don't. Don't do this. Don't let our last time together turn into this. You know as well as I do how this progresses. And I don't want to go through it. I fear that much more than dying. Don't put me through that. If you care about me, you'll understand. And I know you do.

"So, every morning, when Oscar wakes you up before you want to get out of bed, think of me. Also when you change his litter."

Harriet had to pull Oscar out from under the bed. He knew. She stuffed him, howling mournfully, into the carrier, kissed Claire on the forehead, and left the apartment.

And Oscar was not the only one to cry that day.

Forty-six

The desktop was clear. She pulled the bottom right drawer open and removed two files. Yom Kippur. My observance, she thought, not quite kosher, but it fits for me. She liked the rhythm of the day, used it in her own way, a ritual, a reckoning, a way to keep track, to keep herself on track, though she realized that she was not, and had never been, off track. More's the pity, she thought, and shrugged her shoulders.

The last time, this one last time. All in order. Of course.

Untying the blue folder labeled *Will*, she ran her finger down the second page. Equal distribution – ACLU, Planned Parenthood, the JHU School of Public Health and Hygiene General Research Fund. A bit for Charlotte, should they find her. Or when they find her, Claire corrected herself. Viktor, Harriet, co-executors.

She reviewed the information in the second file, phone numbers for her attorney, double checking bank and brokerage account numbers. In order. All in order.

And now, she thought, some thoughts, some goodbyes. Viktor will take care of all of this.

She labelled a third file: *Last Letters* and pulled out the box of Crane's stationary, heavy, off-white, a substantial feel. Claire smiled as she remembered Lily's telling her to always use quality stationery. "It tells who you are without your having to."

So I am telling who I am, she thought, even without the fancy expensive writing paper.

For Annaliese –

Oh, how long it has been since I've seen you, thought of you – yet you are here with me, perhaps always. Your strength, stoicism – how much I learned from you, was influenced by you – though I didn't know it at the time – what a child I was – I cringe to think of it now – I had seen nothing of life, thought my mother's death gave me license to enter that world of those who-have-known-sadness, that I was a fully qualified member of that cohort. And perhaps it did – what, after all, do Americans know of the kinds of tragedies you experienced. So young were you. We know only the personal – we such individuals here –

Now, knowing only a portion, my small, individual ration, of life, I see with different eyes. I have loved someone who has experienced it all -- well, all tragedy is ultimately personal, I guess – and I realized that I loved, and was scared of, you as well. Such depth, such nihilism – it took me years to recognize what you carried, what you radiated? not the right word, not right at all – and how you showed me how naïve, hollow, callow, perhaps, I was – a child who knew nothing of life.

But there was something, must have been something, in me that was drawn to you – a knowledge that I was to be, needed to be, more – and you gave that to me – and I appreciate it beyond measure. Though I do realize that your gift was often wrapped in an insulting condescension – how I appreciate, understand that now – and think how often I have responded to those eager, raw, ambitious young women who now think the world is theirs. How we learn, dearest Annaliese, the sadness that this world has on offer. Only the hard way, yes? Only the hard way.

So, this letter is to thank you, and to tell you that I miss you – am sad that our lives have not touched. I'd always hoped that you would contact me – thought that we would have been, could have been, friends, as equals now. Ah, another sorrow. I remember you called me "little chicken" – that I am no longer – both of us bowed, but not broken, I hope, by life.

Perhaps this letter will one day find you.

Claire

Dear Louisa,

I thought that I would have lots to say to you – a lifetime of stored thoughts, responses, anger. But words, these last words for you, to you, don't seem to be there. For, really, what is there to say at this point?

If I say 'I forgive you,' that, I think, would only enrage you. I know that if you said that to me that would be my response. For I see myself as the innocent here, the victim, collateral damage, though most times not even collateral – I'd say targeted.

And, really, all I wanted to be was loved. More's the pity that you didn't see that. Mamma always thought that I was a bit of a sap in that regard. And, hard as it is to admit it, she was right. She saw that as an essential character flaw in me. I don't know what she saw where you were concerned. Perhaps too much of herself.

I know that you've carried much unhappiness throughout your life, that there is pain behind so much of cruelty, misdirected though it may have been. I have to say that I wish that you would have focused it on someone other than I, but bullies always seem to have a gift for finding the weak and the weak spot – so I see my contribution to that dance. Your anger, my looking for love – what those flaws cost us. What a waste. We are a bit like Baby Jane, without the kitsch.

Well, I thought I'd have nothing to say – seems I do – and bitter – yes, your ever-so-sweet sister is bitter, over what you've done, how you've treated me, disparaged me, hurt me Maybe if I'd told you so earlier, it would have been different. Maybe Mamma was right – you would have respected me more. Not that I'm making this my

194

fault – it isn't. That rests, whatever the reason, with you. So maybe I haven't forgiven you; maybe I'm still angry.

Ah, well, it's done; it's over, both of us scarred and apart. And that is okay with me. Auf Wiedersehen. I'm not sorry we won't meet again.

Oh Mamma – I do wonder what my life would have been had you lived – though not too much different, I suppose – maybe for Louisa, not for me – I was never in that triangle – a blessing – and a sadness, saved from tumult, consigned to loneliness, ever an outsider, though I realize that I was an outsider from – what? pain? No, that is there – always, a longing – ah, at least not as crazy as Louisa – a sad solace, albeit a solace.

I loved you – everything about you- your style, your way with men, with Faht – I realize, see now, that yours was one of those marriages where there was room for only two – at least for you. Louisa must have sensed it, fought against it – more's the pity – for her – and I, well, I guess I just accepted it, and tried to make you love me. I think I succeeded.

Oh, Mamma, this life I've had – I think you would be proud. I don't think you were one for introspection. I wish I weren't. And, no, I'm nowhere near as pretty as you.

Claire

Dearest Charlotte,

I have never forgotten you – how I loved you, sweet little pumpkin – and there is a hole in my heart that always waits for you. I thought I would be jealous, that's what Mamma said – that girls were always jealous – so that when I saw you for the first time and felt my heart open, well, a delightful surprise.

And I do understand – why you left, why you went so far, why, all the whys – and I'm sad – for what you experienced. You mom – well, so much of it wasn't really her fault – though that, knowing that, only helps, doesn't erase. I wish it could have been different. But know that you are loved, you are remembered. Know that I will always be your Clairedelune.

Perhaps one day I will find you.

These are getting harder and harder to write, Claire thought, and put down the pen, until next time.

For Janet Speer

My dear friend,

You, who knew me when. When I was a naïve girl, thinking she was a woman. You helped me grow up, you know. You, with your laughter, your way of looking at life, your freedom. How I admired, and loved, you. And how I loved, and wondered, that you loved me. I still can't see why, but was I ever lucky to have met you, to have had you in my life. You showed me real laughter, gave me a sense of insouciance (I know you will love that I used that word!), and a balance of lightness that I didn't know I needed.

My heart broke when you left, though I do understand why. Because, really, you never left. I had oh so many conversations with you over those years, over these years. To get your take on things. And it is that which has helped me make this decision. I have pondered; I have decided and am - I would never say "at peace" with it – rather, I know that this is the right thing to do, right for me, right for everyone I love.

And I wish you happiness, continued contentment, you deserve that. I guess that sometimes you just get tired. And your free spirit, I think, deserves a bit of a rest. I will never forget you, Naomi. Please do not forget me.

With so much love,

Claire

My dearest, dearest Faht,

I'm not sure why I'm writing this. What is it I can say to you that you wouldn't already know, intuit? I do know that you would understand, support my decision. I do know that you would be sad that I have made it. But ...

So you know how much you have meant to me, how much I have loved, love, you, admire you, emulate you. You were always there, supporting me, encouraging me to step out, to take risks. And I do want you to know that I have thought about you, considered your life, apart from simply being my father. I know that there was more, much more to you. You and Mamma; you and Onkel August; you and Louisa. The last I don't think I'll ever understand – it was, perhaps, the only time you let me down. There. I must say that. Why you allowed her to treat me the way that she did, why you never intervened, never spoke up. Well, perhaps you did. It is for you to know. But it hurt me. I wonder if you knew that, or if you thought that I was just too sweet, too good, too loving, to realize. For a long while I was. And then I stepped back a bit to observe, to see how nothing, no one, really, ever operates alone, without a system that either supports or circumscribes their freedom to act. Ah, so late now, too late now. But I want you to know that it did affect me, in ways that I still carry. So even if one can decipher, define, understand, the deep pain stays, under the surface, ready to surface. The scar, always there, sometimes throbs, no?

So now I've said that, told you. And it's over. But my love, my admiration, my appreciation, overshadows all of that. My loving, handsome, vulnerable Faht. Who could never protect me, but who showed me love and how to love,

Clairedelune

Dear, dear Viktor,

There is really no need for me to write to you, is there? You know it all, my thoughts, my hopes, or nearly all my hopes, dreams, my sadness, fears. You know my decision, the reasons why. And you are one of those reasons, to leave you now, so that you can remember me, remember us, as we were, all that we were.

For, you know, I have loved you as no other. The love of my life. And not perfect, this love, us, not perfect at all. Not quite whole, but there, and more than enough. I have been, have felt, alone all of my life. Except when I was with Faht. And then when I met you. I don't know if there is such a thing as a soulmate. I'm thinking that's much too saccharine for us to even contemplate. But, just in case there is, for those brief moments when we allow ourselves to be sentimental…

You have been a light in my life. And it has been good, hasn't it, for the most part. Good and real and…well, this is not a time for me to get maudlin. You know. You know it all.

So I leave, thinking of, loving, you.

Claire

Forty-seven

When she couldn't manage to swallow her morning coffee, she knew.

And once she knew, she felt an energy that had been missing. Letters written, bills paid, all necessary information provided, drawers straightened. Claire walked through her apartment, paused at each window, touched each piece of furniture, remembering Sylvan Cliffs, Fritz's apartment, her purchases, 90-days-same-as-cash, from Potthast's. Viktor had already left for work, leaving her coffee there, all she had to do was warm it.

Leaning on the back of the chair, her favorite, she savored the views of St. Paul Street, remembering a Saturday morning, a girl in a yellow sweater, who wondered if it just could be possible for her to live in the St. Paul Court Apartments.

Claire turned to the sofa, pulled the phone toward her before she sat down. She dialed, Harriet, hoping that she would be home, that this could be a quiet time for them. She knew what she wanted to say.

Harriet picked up on the fourth ring.

"Is this a good time?" Claire said, relieved that her voice sounded strong to her ears. It did not to Harriet's.

"Claire," she answered, "what can I do for you? Company?"

But Claire had had enough company; she wanted their last meeting to remain that. "No, no company, just a chat. And no tears. If I hear tears, I'm hanging up, and you don't want that."

"No. we have learned to be good soldiers. If nothing else." Harriet bit down hard on her index finger. She knew what was coming.

Claire tried to swallow, and, unable to, wiped her mouth with her handkerchief. She continued, as best she could; her words, she knew, would be garbled. I should have called earlier, she thought.

"So, it's soon now. And I wanted one last goodbye."

Harriet could find no words in response.

Claire cleared her throat. Better, she thought. "And I want you to know that I have no worries. Once my decision was made, finally made, there was nothing more to worry about. And I'm grateful for that.

"And regrets, I've spent time thinking about that too. but any are small when I think of what I've had in my life. You among them, dear friend."

Harriet held her forehead, took deep breaths to keep the tears under control.

"Now I said 'no crying,' right?"

Harriet nodded silently.

"So kiss Oscar for me, will you? Every morning."

Harriet opened her mouth to speak, but Claire had ended the call.

The Last Chapter

It was in her mind before she woke, always there, just under the surface. Viktor had wanted to stay, but she wanted this last night to herself. "We've spent enough nights together," she told him. "Let's remember those. This, well, this would only make the memory, the last memory, sad. And we've had enough of that for this life, don't you think?"

He had taken her hand and kissed it, then left without saying another word.

He would arrive, earlier, she knew, than they had agreed upon. She was grateful for that. She rose, splashed cold water on her face, then looked in the mirror and laughed. She smoothed her eyebrows. Today I'm looking pretty good. It figures. She said these last two words aloud, and was glad.

She took care when she dressed, chose a favorite black cashmere sweater, although black was not the most becoming color for her these days; a pleated Stewart-tartan skirt, complete with oversized safety pin, a bit too young for her, a bit too big on her now slight frame. But it was a favorite. And black hose, black patent-leather flats, with a black grosgrain bow. Yes, this was how she wanted to look. She brushed her hair back, and with all that had befallen her, still mourned that it was no longer thick, that, if she looked, she could see her skull. What does Viktor see, she wondered, and then closed her eyes.

She wanted to be fully present this day, to experience this day, with Viktor. Books, music, they had spent many of their precious hours planning it. And ice cream, Hendler's Vanilla Bean, topped with bourbon. She had planned; all that needed to be taken care of was taken care of. No loose ends, no one to leave them to anyway, except Viktor. He would handle what needed to be handled.

He arrived, an hour earlier than they had agreed upon. He always knocked, three rapid raps, before he used the key he had possessed for years. His favorite books, favorite records already part of her, their, collection.

They sat through the afternoon, left the lamps unlit as the evening came, nursed their drinks, from habit. Their ritual, important on this day, to both. They read, each with their own thoughts, but close, sitting close, on the sofa. Later Claire lay, her head in Viktor's lap as he stroked her forehead. She reached for his hand and placed it on her chest.

"It's time, I think." She spoke without looking at him, and started to sit up.

He helped her as she raised her head, her shoulders, from his lap. "I need to tell you," he said, as he leaned her body against his. "I'm going with you. We'll do this together." He put his fingers to her lips. "Don't waste, don't use your energy talking about this. If you are not here, then I have no life, no life that I am interested in living. How many deaths have I escaped? This is one I don't want to. We'll go. We'll go together."

Claire shook her head. "Agata. What about Agata?" She was so tired, couldn't muster up energy to say words she knew should be said.

"Agata. Another sad soul. But she knew, from the beginning she knew. And decided on what she wanted. Another broken soul, Claire, just one more. She will be relieved, I think. This has been no life for her, not really. She has friends, people who love her. They'll make her life better." Viktor took her hand, kissed it. "She knew, Claire. She always knew."

They sat, each with only thoughts, words insufficient, or unnecessary, now. She knew, Claire thought. Yes, she knew. And Viktor, my love, will do exactly as he chooses. I was, I am his love, she thought. Yes, it is I.

They walked to the bedroom, Viktor steadying her gait. He helped her onto the bed, straightened the coverlet, fluffed the pillows behind her. She reached into the drawer of the bedside table, pulled out the containers of sleeping pills. She had been accumulating them for months. "I think ice cream now. Would you fix it?"

Viktor went into the kitchen, spooned two scoops into the two bowls Claire had chosen, emptied the capsules and added enough morphine to do what it was meant to do. He added a spoonful of bourbon to each, for taste, and the memory.

Returning, he handed one dish to Claire, then got into bed on his customary side. After a few bites, Claire looked over. "Make sure I get all this down." She paused. "I know this is the right thing for me, the right ending." She stared into the bowl. "And you? Are you sure?"

Viktor smiled, scraped the last of the liquid onto his spoon.

"Now don't forget to wash the bowls and put them in the dish drainer."

Viktor smiled. "Ah, yes. We will follow our plan."

"And make sure that we're sitting up. In case things get messy. I would hate that."

"No worry. No worry. My Clairedelune."

He returned from the kitchen and took her hand. Her breathing had slowed; he knew his would soon follow suit.

"But who will be the executor? Who will take care of all the details? We shouldn't leave that to Harriet. It isn't fair. I, we, haven't prepared her for this."

Viktor took her hand, leaned to kiss her forehead. "Oh, my Clairedelune. Some things you just have to leave to chance."

Claire smiled and closed her eyes, feeling her hand in his, and thought of Viktor, of Fritz, of Lily, of Sylvan Cliffs, and General.

Made in the USA
Columbia, SC
12 October 2020